FAKE IT

till you make it

A NOVEL

BRIANNA RAE QUINN

Hardbound ISBN: 978-1-7356362-2-1

Paperback ISBN: 978-1-7356362-3-8

eBook ISBN: 978-1-7356362-4-5

For Nick --

the man who chose to love me through everything.

CHAPTER ONE

Tick, Tock, Tick, Tock, the clock's metronome whipped the students' ears in the final minutes of class before they would be freed for the weekend. A chorus of zippers buzzed one after another as students packed their bags, preparing to make a dash for their busses, while others decompressed, tossing quips back and forth, musing over their weekend plans.

At the far left of the classroom, facing the windows, a group of three girls sat casually, absent-mindedly fidgeting with their cell phones while their teacher pretended not to notice and packed her own bag with stacks of assignments, haphazardly piled on top of one another by the careless students in her unmotivated chemistry class.

Violet twisted locks of her long blonde hair between her fingers, which was somewhat more interesting to her than listening to her friends bicker about boys and failing the Bechdel test. She blew stray hairs out of her eyes, listening and waiting for the right time to speak, as she so often did.

"My parents are taking me camping," the feminine voice of her taller friend, Yvonne, huffed as she sat on one of the long, black lab tables coiling around the room. She kicked one leg back and forth, setting her phone down. She had obviously grown bored of whatever stared back at her on the screen.

"Don't act all mad," the last girl, Emmy, replied. "You'll probably see that guy again." She gave a mischievous smirk. She leaned from her chair over the table, moving her glasses further down her nose as if to imply she didn't need them to see through her friend's pseudo-frustration.

"Have you been talking to him?" Violet questioned.

The tall girl very subtly blushed but tried to play it cool. "Yeah, but he's been kind of awkward, I guess." She grabbed her phone again, and sat forward, opening a series of text messages from a contact titled 'Steven'.

She scrolled to the top, and the girls all scanned through the short exchange of messages on the screen.

MAYBE: STEVEN
hi, yvonne… its steven.

YVONNE
Hi :)

STEVEN
u goin up again this weekend…?

YVONNE
Yeah. You?

STEVEN
yeah…

Violet dropped her hair from her fingers, making a face."Yeah, that's super awkward. Dot, dot dot." She chuckled at her own joke.

Yvonne rolled her eyes and returned her phone to her eyes only. "I think he's expecting something to, like, you know, happen this weekend."

Emmy pushed her glasses up her nose and hopped onto the table beside Yvonne and snatched the phone out of her hands, pretending to type in the text box, "Steven, I look forward to seeing you again, as

I'm sure you'll look forward to seeing me naked in my tent tonight. PS. If you have any hot, single brothers, my friend, Emmy is completely available."

Yvonne snatched her phone from Emmy's palms as the dismissal bell finally rang, and a wave of students pushed into the hallway, practically racing to get out of the building.

A few stragglers remained in the classroom, including the trio of ladies. Violet rose from her chair, only half listening to her friends teasing each other as she threw her backpack over her shoulder.

"Vi, do you need a ride home?" Emmy asked, finally realizing she was preparing to walk away.

"Nah," Violet responded. "Jess is taking me home today. I guess Spirit Club got canceled or something."

"Okay then, I'll text you later." She began to grab her own things with Yvonne close behind.

Violet exited her classroom to a noticeably empty hallway. So far, the best part of her junior year at Northridge High School was knowing she didn't have to risk an elbow to the face in an over-crowded hallway as she sprinted to make it to her bus on time. She firmly believed that the five minutes the school gave to board the busses after school was entirely too short a window.

As she walked, she wondered if Yvonne would really go through with seeing this guy, Steven, over the weekend.

Yvonne was always their pretty friend. She was tall and thin and really had the sort of model body type that the health teachers always told the class shouldn't be idolized because it's just "not real." She had this gorgeous, dark, curly hair that always seemed to fall so perfectly, it was like every time she flicked her hair out of her eyes it was in slow motion.

For that reason, boys loved her. She always had a date for homecoming before the theme was even announced, and she drew tons of attention any time they'd go out for ice cream together.

Emmy and Violet were usually the middle-men, dropping off phone numbers written on the backs of receipts or used napkins or telling some stranger's wingman whether she was available.

Incidentally, she usually was. Yvonne wasn't the type who was super comfortable being alone with boys, she found she never really knew what to say. Emmy frequently teased her, finding it so ironic that the "hot one" of their friend group would be so awkward and hesitant to really go on any dates.

Somehow, this guy seemed different to her. Violet noticed how much more frequently Yvonne had been going camping with her family. They're quite athletic and outdoorsy, and ever since the summer, she'd had her eyes on a boy whose family always seemed to be a few spots away, just within view from their fire pit.

It took weeks of reports of prolonged eye-contact from across the lake, or noticing him showing off on his bike down the trail before she finally spoke to him for the first time (a casual "hey" in passing outside the bathroom), and even longer still from them before they finally exchanged phone numbers.

Violet listened to cute stories of the two of them stargazing and brushing hands nearly every week, in which Emmy liked to insert herself, embellishing with lewd commentary or assumptions, claiming her version of events would be far more exciting, and lamenting on how Yvonne really needed to take some notes on her creative dialogue to get to the "fun stuff" a bit more promptly.

Fake It till You Make It

If this was the weekend her friend would truly lose her virginity, Violet would be the only one left with a wholly unpopped cherry. She imagined Emmy bringing up this point, and suddenly turning her focus from Yvonne to her: Virgin Violet.

Part of her knew, of course, that this may have been some wild idea born from her constant overthinking. Violet was the logical one of her group. She was very much a think-before-you-speak type of person, overanalytical and calculated. She thought this was both a blessing and a curse; she always felt confident in her choices, but that also meant problems would swirl around in her head for hours or days until the solutions came.

She shook the thoughts out of her head and removed her phone from the back pocket of her jeans, sliding upward on the screen to open her collection of text messages from her good friend Jess.

Jess was a senior this year, and easily one of the most well-known students at the school, for better and for worse. She was incredibly outspoken, but cared a lot about the student body and her friends (that might be why she wound up as student council vice president.) She also happened to be Violet's neighbor, and as such she offered Violet rides home on the days she wasn't too busy after school.

JESS

Grabbing something from the main office. Meet you at the back entrance.

Violet replied with a thumbs-up emoji and followed her usual path down to the back entrance of the high school leading out to the student parking lot.

She placed herself on a bench in the anteroom between the two sets of doors that led into the school, waiting for her friend to appear. Outside of the glass doors, she watched the parking lot slowly empty like the air from a balloon, leaving a flat patch of concrete behind. She counted the cars remaining as she waited until she heard the first set of doors open behind her.

She looked over her shoulder to see two familiar boys entering the vestibule. They were Xander and Travis, two friends from math class. "Hey," she called to them with a smile.

The boys turned and waved. "Hey," Xander returned before they approached her bench. "Waiting on a ride?" he asked.

"Sort of," Violet replied, looking back from where the boys came to see if she could spot Jess hustling through the corridor to meet her. She was met with no such sight, only the metaphorical rolling tumbleweeds that exist in schools over the weekend. "My friend is picking something up from the office, then she's taking me home."

Travis stood, propped against the door, indicating his desire to go, but Xander didn't follow his lead. Instead, he continued their conversation. "Ah. So you doing anything fun this weekend?"

Xander was one of Violet's oldest friends at Northridge High. They had met during freshman year and became quite close, even dating for a few months before mutually deciding they were better off as friends; it was about as ideal as a first breakup could have been for a fourteen-year-old

, and now at sixteen, they enjoyed each other's company and stayed in close contact.

"Not really." Violet shrugged, still looking and waiting for Jess's silhouette to appear down the hallway. "Yvonne's going camping, and Emmy's grounded," she explained.

"What did she do this time?" Travis asked, knowing the story must be good.

Emmy was the wild-card friend, the one who often danced so close to the line she'd nearly cross it. She liked to claim it was her super strict parents that made her such a rebellious spirit, and the fact that they were easy to trick that made her so prone to adventure. All of this was reported as she gulped down massive swigs of Malibu straight from the bottle she found in her parents' basement, naturally.

"I guess her parents installed some spyware on her computer after the last incident. They caught her talking to some twenty-four-year-old guy who lives across the country."

"Oh, come on. Everyone's done that," Xander noted.

"Yeah, well, she's not one to leave out any lurid details. It was pretty graphic," Violet added.

"Graphic how? Like pictures?" Travis wondered aloud, suddenly interested in the passing conversation, and peeling himself off the glass door to get in closer.

Violet chuckled. "She said she sent pictures, but they weren't of her. Either way, her parents were not amused."

The boys both laughed along with her.

Travis checked his watch and looked out at his car, baking in the parking lot. "Well," he started, "just because you losers don't have anything planned for this weekend doesn't mean I don't. I'm taking Lindsey out for her birthday tonight and I got to shave," he said, angling a thumb over his shoulder to his old beater of a car in the back of the lot, barely visible out the window.

Xander and Violet exchanged a glance, looking intently at his bare face without a single noticeable strand of facial hair.

Travis noticed them analyzing his face and quickly stroked an invisible beard, before amending his previous statement with a simple, "If you know what I mean."

Violet nodded slowly as Xander waved his hands in front of him as if to say he needn't say any more. The message was received.

Xander returned his gaze to Violet and quickly changed the subject. "My parents are going out of town to visit my brother at his college, so I'll be pretty bored all weekend. If you want, we can hang out or something?"

Violet thought for a moment and then nodded. "Yeah, maybe."

"I'll text you?" He offered, as Travis began edging toward the door to leave, obviously irritated with the continued chatter.

She nodded again and smiled, waving her goodbye to the boys as they filtered through the doorway.

She watched them walk away, recalling Travis' hairlessness and sighing as she leaned back into her bench seat. So far, this was her least favorite part of junior year at Northridge High school. All anyone ever talked about now was sex.

Every party turned from casually hanging around in someone's basement became a game of Seven Minutes in Heaven, or spin the bottle with increasingly high stakes the more you landed on the same person. Never Had I Ever turned into uncomfortable silence as her peers struggled to consider things they had yet to do, or worse, turned into a competition to figure out who had done the most.

Violet never paid much mind to the hype. She played the games and laughed along with others when they made their dirty jokes, but it just never seemed to make sense to spend a lot of time or energy thinking about sex, especially considering her relationship status had been consistently single since her relationship with Xander over a year ago. Now, however, she seemed to notice sex becoming more and more prevalent everywhere she went.

Violet's eyes returned to her hands, twisting her phone around in her lap as she waited a bit longer for her friend to push through the doors.

Her fingers tingled from a pulsing vibration from her phone. She unlocked the screen to be greeted with something rather reassuring—

JESS
Sorry. Coming now.

And as she looked up, she noticed her friend finally appear around the corner so her weekend could begin.

CHAPTER TWO

"What's wrong?" Violet asked as Jess plowed through the first set of doors, her braids seeming to weigh her down. She looked disheveled and frankly, a bit thrown off. Her dark eyes flashed with pure irritation, but it was speckled with hints of worry rather than pure anger. The tension was already palpable as she continued walking right past Violet, holding the next door open for her, obviously eager to get away.

"Come on, I'll tell you in the car," Jess groaned.

Violet noticed a sheet of paper folded up in Jess's hand as she pulled the strap of her bag over her shoulder again, preparing to follow her friend outside. She wanted to ask some more specific questions but decided it was best to wait.

Fake It till You Make It

The two friends hiked through the lot over to a dirty, black sedan, sitting alone in one of the farthest rows of parking spaces. Jess opened her dusty trunk and tossed her backpack, keeping the sheet of paper clutched in her fist. Violet slid into the passenger seat and shoved her bag between her knees on the floor while Jess slammed her trunk closed. It didn't always close so easily, but something about this slam and the way it rumbled through the entire vehicle felt a little too intentional.

Violet grew anxious; it wasn't often that Jess got so visibly distraught. She was normally quite put together and rarely lost her cool, especially because she needed to have a certain amount of credibility with both her peers and the administration. Violet always imagined her friend would go far into politics ever since their younger days. She had the strongest opinions on everything, and while she wasn't always the type to scream them the loudest, she would most definitely scream longer and more intelligently than the loudest guy. Taking a leadership role in the student council was right for her.

This demeanor she had on was directly contradictory to her usual reputation, and as Jess forced her driver's side door shut and twisted the key to start her car, Violet still couldn't bring herself to ask again. She decided it was best to wait until Jess either calmed down a little or brought it up herself.

She still, however, couldn't help but notice as Jess stuffed the folded sheet of paper from her hand into the front cupholder, wondering once again if that unassuming white sheet had anything to do with the sudden weight of the space around them.

The radio lights blinked and began blasting some upbeat disco-pop music that made the atmosphere in the car that much more awkward. Violet took note of the juxtaposition between the look on their faces and the positive tune that played behind them. The joints in her fingers flexed back and forth as she nervously awaited the apparent, imminent blow-up from her typically calm and collected friend.

Finally, as they pulled out of the now deserted parking lot, Jess reached over and turned the volume down to only a whisper as she sighed, keeping her eyes set dead ahead on the road in front of them.

Exasperated, Violet also let out a breath. She felt as though she'd been holding it in this whole time. "What happened?"

"Remember that conference I went to last weekend?"

"Yeah…" Violet trailed off, unsure of where this conversation might have been heading toward. The conference was a relatively major event, with several local high schools getting together to discuss fundraising events and collaborating on common issues going on in each school to effectively solve them. It always seemed like a smart idea to Violet, though she never had much interest in attending — the experience of being a part of one high school community was enough.

"Well, when I was there, a bunch of students from Southeast High School and their advisor did this really cool panel on niche clubs and forming communities or support for high school students in minor groups, sort of like a safe-space for discussions about possible mistreatment and creating direct lines of communication between those communities and the administration."

Violet listened intently, still wondering how something that seemed so good could lead to her being so upset. Jess continued.

"Southeast High said they just adopted a new club last year called the Gay-Straight Alliance. They call it their GSA, to address misconceptions about the LGBTQ+ community, provide education and resources, and just general support, and as I was thinking about it, I realized we don't really have any support for students with different sexual orientations in the school. It seemed like such a good thing, so I got the contact information for the advisor, and their student council representatives and I was chatting with them this week and they encouraged me to get the paperwork started to get a GSA on our club roster ASAP. So I went in to get the request form to start a new club today."

Violet glanced down at the paper, curled around itself in the cup holder. That must have been the form. She could understand how Jess could have gotten upset if something had gone wrong. Her passion often led her to get rather emotionally attached to her projects. She continued to listen intently.

"I asked one of the secretaries about the form, and she started asking me what kind of club I was hoping to start. I told her about the conference and all that, and she just had the nastiest face on. It got so awkward and I just kept talking and trying to explain and all this and she was looking at me like I had three damn heads! I just couldn't—" she stopped herself and took a deep breath.

"So I finished, and she's just staring at me, and I'm like, 'Is there a problem with that?' and she said," Jess stopped a moment and put on this annoyingly high-pitched, condescending tone, "I just don't think that's going to go well. I doubt the school will approve of instituting such a controversial club."

Suddenly, her anger and frustration made sense, and tons of thoughts went flooding through Violet's head. Violet was certain she wasn't gay, but absolutely supported any person who wanted to live their most authentic life and love who they love. At this time in America, it seemed ridiculous that anyone could be so hateful and discouraging. She wanted to share these thoughts, but again, she chose to sit and listen while Jess unloaded her feelings of disappointment onto her passenger. She was sure Jess would share her sentiments.

"First of all, I can't even believe a school employee had the audacity to discourage any student looking to take on a leadership opportunity like starting a new club, and second of all, I don't understand how this is even a point of controversy! I know for a fact there are gay students in that school who are being bullied for something that is completely not their choice, and this woman had the nerve to tell me it would be an issue to provide a support system for that!? I was seething! There is absolutely no room for that kind of homophobic behavior from an authority figure in a place of learning. I'm just appalled, and disgusted, and—and…" she punctuated her thoughts with a poignant groan.

There was then a moment of silence, backed only by the quiet whispers of some radio talk-show hosts still playing and laughing from the speakers, blissfully unaware of how inappropriately their chuckles filled the pause between these two listeners. By this point, Jess was tense all over. Her shoulders were practically up to her ears, and her grip on the steering wheel made her knuckles white.

Violet looked away from Jess's face and looked out the window. They were stopped at a red light, still a good few minutes from home. As much as she wanted to yell along with her, she and Jess were very similar when their blood began to boil. They needed to get their frustrations out quickly and explosively in a safe space so they could refocus more rationally.

"That sucks," was all that Violet managed to say. There was nothing meaningful to add to Jess's tirade. She just wanted her to know she had been heard.

Jess's breathing slowed a bit, and the air in the car felt a little lighter. It was likely that all the anger had filtered out of her system and she was ready to move onto a new topic to distract her from the struggles that may come with establishing her new club. She glanced over at Violet. "It's fine. I'll figure it out." There was a pause. "Are you doing anything fun this weekend?" The light turned green and they proceeded down the road.

Violet shrugged. "A lot of my friends are busy this weekend. Yvonne is going camping; Emmy is grounded. I did run into Travis and Xander while I was waiting for you, and Xander said his parents are going to visit his brother this weekend, so maybe I'll spend some time with him."

"Yeah? Your dad's going to let him over?" She let out a scoff disguised as a laugh to show her skepticism. Xander was the only boy that Violet had really dated in the last few years since her parents got divorced, and Mr. Gray, like the protective single father he was, didn't much care for his daughter to have boys around the house, even if he was with them.

"Well, he actually invited me over to his place."

Jess raised an eyebrow. "So you'll be alone in his house with no parents and no siblings then?"

"I guess."

Another pause.

"Is Travis going to be there?"

Violet suddenly felt as though she were in an interrogation. "I don't know. He said he was taking his girlfriend out for her birthday tonight. He didn't say anything about the rest of the weekend."

"Hm," the sound left Jess's closed lips with her eyebrows quickly rising before settling once again.

Violet just looked at her as she stared down the road, pressing her to explain herself a little further. What was she implying?

"What?"

"Nothing, I just think," she took a moment to carefully consider her words before saying, "You know I think he's still a little into you and I know you're close with him, I just don't want him to get any ideas if you do actually decide to go to his place knowing it's just going to be the two of you."

Violet loosely crossed her arms, feeling a sour taste in the back of her throat from the insinuation. As much as Jess had a point, she was certain Xander respected her enough to not push too far if she wasn't comfortable, but she'd always been comfortable with him. She trusted him.

"I appreciate the concern, but I'm sure it will be fine. We're just really close, besides, you know me," she spoke slowly, "I'm not really in a rush in that particular department. I have no problems waiting until I'm ready."

"Really? It seems like it's all you and your friends talk about."

"Well, yeah, but that's just a part of being in high school, isn't it? Everyone's getting their cars, parents are leaving their kids alone for the weekend because they're 'mature enough' now or whatever. I don't know." She dropped her hands and started picking at a hangnail on her thumb. "It makes sense with all the opportunities, I guess."

Jess shrugged, making the turn into their neighborhood. "I'm not trying to tell you what to do, but as obsessed as everyone is with losing their virginity, I don't want you to regret losing it to someone random, and especially someone you've already decided is not boyfriend material."

"I wasn't even thinking about having sex with him. Honestly, do you really think he's going to make a move like that?"

"I have no clue, Vi. You know him better than I do, I guess. I can't even imagine what goes through a hormonal teenage boy's brain, and to say the least I think I'd be shocked if I could." She offered a smile to lighten the mood.

Violet let out a quick snort. When she thought about it, Jess was right. Emmy was the most suggestive friend she had, and she'd already lost her virginity. What must be going on in the mind of a guy who didn't even know what it was like? She had some guesses from the handful of *Cosmopolitan* magazines she'd flipped through in the supermarket. According to those "sexperts", anticipation made the experience better, which was why there always seemed to be articles with the top five or six sultry messages to send your man while he's at work for the "Best Sex of Your Life™."

She made a face to herself, refocusing just in time for Jess to pull into the driveway outside of her house. Her dad was pushing the lawnmower through the side yard of the house with headphones in his ears as Jess put the car into park.

Violet grabbed her backpack from between her legs and sat it on her lap. She pushed her door open to exit the car, looking back over at Jess. "Thanks for the ride," she said, "and let me know if you need any help with the GSA stuff. I think you're right, the school really needs something like that."

CHAPTER THREE

As Violet headed up the paved driveway to the open garage, she raised her arm to wave at her dad so he would notice she had come home. He smiled and waved back before she disappeared behind the walls of the garage.

Her parents had divorced while she was in middle school, though it never really seemed to bother her. She noticed the signs. Her dad was sleeping in the basement, her mom never called him for dinner, and by the time they sat Violet down to tell her they planned to separate, she only nodded and said "Okay."

She was never particularly close to her mom. Mrs. Gray often worked late and got easily overwhelmed at home, so after the divorce when she told Violet she would be moving out-of-state to take a new, well-paying job, the conversation was rather brief. Violet loved her mom, of course, but even at thirteen, she was one to approach things rationally and reasonably.

She hopped over a pile of junk on the floor on her way into the house. The garage was "organized chaos", as her dad called it. She noticed the empty plot of cement flooring from which the lawnmower had been moved and laughed to herself, thinking how silly it was that the small corner was now the cleanest part of the Gray family garage.

She swung open the door from the garage that led straight into the kitchen and felt the breeze as it quickly slammed shut behind her. The straps on her backpack practically jumped off her shoulders onto the floor beside the kitchen table, and Violet went straight for the fridge to grab an apple before settling up on the chair beside her bag and scrolling aimlessly through social media posts on her phone.

Mostly, she wanted to get the thought of what Jess had said about Xander out of her head. She didn't often think about her virginity (or having sex at all) unless someone brought it up first, which, as she noticed, became a more and more frequent occurrence. By all counts, her friends seemed to care more about her sex life than she did.

But what if Jess was right? What if Xander was in the same boat as she was? Travis was obviously doing the deed with his girlfriend. Maybe he just wanted to lose his virginity to get his friends to leave him alone about it.

Violet continued scrolling through her phone. She had noticed a few pictures of impossibly skinny women in bikinis, straddling their supermodel boyfriends with washboard abs on the beach. She scrolled past them with an exasperated sigh; she couldn't do anything without being reminded of sex.

If Xander was planning on making a move, would that be such a bad idea? Violet knew that this was all Jess's speculation, the chance that she was right about the reason Xander invited her over seemed rather slim. The two of them had spent plenty of time alone together in the past year, though to be fair, it was usually in the form of walking to a fast food place after school or carpooling to football games. She suddenly realized she'd never spent any time with him completely alone and in private since they dated.

Maybe he did want to make a move, and if he did, maybe it was kind of genius?

Violet stopped scrolling on a photo of a Kardashian. She wasn't sure which sister it was, but she knew it was certainly one of them. The woman sat facing away from the camera with her arms around herself and her feet in what was probably a pool or hot tub. She wore a pair of thong-style bikini bottoms hiked up past her hips and no top so her slightly wet hair fell over her bare shoulders. The photo reminded her a lot of the stack of magazines she'd found in the chaos of the garage when she was looking for a screwdriver. Once again, everything led her mind back to sex.

Violet sighed and tapped her way out of the app, taking a final bite of her apple before tossing away the core and moving into the den. She sat herself down on the sofa in the center of the room, snatching the remote from the floor where it had likely fallen as she went.

She pressed the power button and waited as the red light turned blue and the screen loaded up. If Xander wanted to shed himself of his virgin status, as he didn't have a girlfriend, it really made a lot of sense to want to take that step with a close friend. There was no risk of it ruining their romantic relationship because they didn't have one; they were both new to the act so it might be easier to get past the awkward parts. Not to mention, they had maintained a good friendship even after the breakup. If she was going to lose her virginity, why *not* do it with Xander?

Jess said she might regret it, but she suddenly wasn't so sure. She wouldn't have to worry about being "Virgin Violet", especially if Yvonne actually went through with seeing Steven that weekend. The overthinking had begun. Her head felt as though it was being pumped up like a deflated basketball, asking herself over and over if she was actually considering having sex just to appease some mild insecurity.

She attempted to distract herself. The TV shone into Violet's eyes as the screen revealed an advertisement for a reality show that would be airing this weekend. Various clips highlighted the more exciting parts of the episode, focusing in on a woman and a man aggressively shoving their tongues into each other's mouths before that same woman started handing out roses to a whole group of men, handsomely dressed in blazers and ties. Another reminder.

Violet clicked the guide button and once again began scrolling for something else while her head pounded. She trusted Xander. If there was anyone who would be right to deflower her any time soon, it would have to be him. Better him than some frat guy in college that she'd *definitely* regret. Maybe this was a good idea.

Finally, she came across a channel playing cartoons—that seemed innocent and comforting, plus a little nostalgia never hurt anyone. She watched as a yellow sea-sponge ran across the screen with his pink starfish friend following close behind. He seemed to be dressed as a girl in this episode. All the other sea creatures made googly eyes at the starfish as he walked by in his wig and a little crop top. It seemed so weird the creators would demonstrate such arousal in an animation for children. The fish held the door open for him, gave him jobs, and asked him out to dinner. By the end it was revealed who the smoking hot starfish babe truly was as he ripped off his wig and clothes, standing in the nude before a crowd of overly excited sea creatures. Sex.

Violet laid herself down on the couch as she watched, tired after the long day. Her eyes drooped slightly as she wondered if it would be so terrible if she took a brief nap to stop rationalizing this wild idea she was having.

Her eyes fully closed as repetitive laughter rang in her ears from the sponge on the TV. She felt herself sinking into a dream when a buzz sounded loudly from the table.

She popped her head up and looked over the back of the couch to the kitchen table where she'd left her phone. It only buzzed once, that meant she had a text message.

It could be from Emmy complaining about something her parents did or said when she got home, or it might be Xander trying to create some more concrete plans for the weekend. She wondered if either of those options was worth having to get up and walk over to the kitchen again. It took a little longer to decide than she would have liked to admit, but she propped herself up and made her way over to the table.

It was Emmy.

EMMY

Moms making me weed the garden with her
lol Happy Friday!!

Violet smiled, trying to imagine what
Emmy's mother may have said to justify this
punishment.

VIOLET

That's what happens when you
can't be trusted with the computer,
Esmerelda. Some sunlight will do
you good.

EMMY

Wow, it's like you were there.

Before Violet had time to respond, her phone
buzzed in her hands again, this time with a text from
Xander.

XANDER

Hey :)

VIOLET

Hey!

She wanted to add something a little more
clever.

VIOLET
Finished helping Travis shave?

XANDER
LOL yup. What you up to?

Violet looked back at the couch longingly, considering the nap that could have been before returning her attention to the phone.

Then she thought, maybe with the right set of messages, she could get a better read on the situation. Again, there was no guarantee that Jess was right.

She thought back to the article she read in *Cosmo* about dirty texts. Maybe she didn't need to go all out, but she could probably spare something subtle and suggestive. With a few modifications, she sent one.

VIOLET
I just took a little nap. Had a dream
about you :)

He didn't respond immediately. Violet suddenly felt her stomach drop. This obviously was not the right move.

She set her phone down on the table again and ran her fingers through her hair.

"Why would I do that?" She asked herself under the breath, tensing and untensing her fingers to hopefully ease some of the anxiety slowly filling her body up from her toes.

Her phone vibrated the table. She could have sworn she felt it move the floor, and that slow feeling of liquid anxiety suddenly felt like a whole bucket flipped over, topping the anxiety off at a new high, even past where her head stopped.

She reached for her phone and flipped it over quickly, not unlocking, but reading the preview message on her home screen.

XANDER
Really? :) what happened?

Violet thought about waiting a little bit to not seem too eager but decided against it. She usually responded rather quickly, and the last thing she wanted to do right now was seem suspicious or out of character.

VIOLET
Just you and me, hanging out alone
at your place.

She felt good about adding that "alone" in there. She smirked, silently dubbing herself the master of subtlety.

XANDER
Right ;) when do you think you want to come over?

The winky face. That had to mean something. She was sure of it. The odds of Jess being right increased exponentially by the second, and the sudden realization that maybe she would come out of this weekend a changed person hit her like a ton of bricks.

She turned her attention to the clock on the oven. Not that night, that'd be too soon. She needed time to prepare, mentally *and* physically. Suddenly she was wondering if she should grab a new razor from the package in the upstairs bathroom— obviously shaving was an important step for preparation.

Fake It till You Make It

At that moment, the garage door swung open and Violet jumped a little at the thought of her dad walking into the room while she was even *thinking* about meeting a boy at his house alone. She quickly typed out another message before shoving her phone in her back pocket—hiding the evidence.

VIOLET
Tomorrow afternoon?

"Hey, sweetie! How was school today?" Mr. Gray announced, wiping beads of sweat off his forehead as he went to the fridge for a bottle of water.

Violet shrugged. "Fine, nothing crazy." She felt a stinging on her tongue, holding back the thoughts in her head. She thought it would be best to talk about something other than herself right now, plus then maybe her dad wouldn't press her for details about the day. "Jess is trying to start a club, but the secretary gave her a hard time because she thinks it's too controversial."

"What's the club?" Mr. Gray looked at her after taking a huge gulp of water.

"It's like a support group for students with different sexual orientations. I guess the bullying has gotten pretty bad this year."

"Oh. Yeah, I can imagine." Mr. Gray was a generally progressive man, though his only regular interaction with any member of the LGBTQ+ community was a gay coworker, Dan. Even with his limited experience, he had seen first hand the difficulties Dan dealt with on a daily basis, and that was coming from grown men.

A vibration came from Violet's pocket.

XANDER
Cool. Come over any time after 12

"Planning anything fun this weekend?" Violet's dad asked, reclaiming his daughter's attention from her phone.

"Um, yeah. I think I'm going to meet some friends for lunch tomorrow," she replied quickly, circumventing the truth. While her dad attempted to continue their conversation, her mind lay elsewhere.

It wasn't long before she'd skirted around the corner and hustled upstairs for her razor.

CHAPTER FOUR

The next morning, Violet woke up to an incessant *tap, tap, tap* of raindrops falling on her window. She sat up quickly and pushed the curtain away from the glass to peer outside. It was gray and raining slightly.

She wondered if that might be a bad omen, but promptly ignored the thought. She was already anxious, she didn't need superstitions making it any worse.

She yawned and stretched. It was about a quarter to ten. That gave her about two hours.

Downstairs, her father sat watching the television and sipping from a coffee mug. Violet had never been a fan of coffee, but she liked the idea of starting the morning off with something hot on a rainy day. She wanted a little something to make the morning feel more special and set a more positive tone for the day.

She called "Good morning, Dad," as she sifted through their kitchenware, searching for a small metal teapot.

Her eyes lay on the TV screen from the kitchen as she filled her pot with warm water from the tap and sat it on the stovetop to boil. A variety of commercials danced across the screen. As she watched, a strange advertisement for a cleaning brand had their bald mascot mopping floors and shaking his hips for a woman biting her lip sensually off to the side.

Violet's eyebrows narrowed at the absurdity of the idea, but as they say, sex sells.

That's about when her teapot started squealing from behind her, and she poured the boiling water into her favorite mug and sipped on a good black tea, agonizing over what was to come. How would it start? Would he initiate it? Would she? What if nothing happened at all?

Regardless, she had prepared a bit the night before. She shaved until she was nearly hairless (deciding to leave her arm hairs intact), she moisturized and chose to use a facemask Yvonne had given her for her birthday over the summer. It had been sitting at the bottom of the drawer in her bathroom, waiting for the right occasion to be used. This had seemed like the right time.

Once she finished her tea, she moved upstairs to her bathroom and began taking out the braids she'd slept in the night before and brushing out the tangles.

She found herself making faces in the mirror, pouting her lips as she adjusted her hair from around her face, to behind the ears, and up to a loose ponytail. Was any one hairstyle sexier than the other? She was thankful in this moment to not have any siblings, or she might have felt more embarrassed.

She decided on putting it up, pulling out some loose strands, and popping some concealer under her eyes, and some liner on her waterline. She leaned over the counter and really looked at herself closely, her nose only inches from the mirror, scrutinizing every visible pore and wrinkle. Her skin had always been relatively clear, save for one or two rather noticeable blemishes. She had one on her chin and one over her right eyebrow. She dabbed it with concealer and popped on some mascara to open up her eyes a bit more. Her eyes were deep brown which gave her a somewhat doe-eyed look as her black pupils made very little contrast. Looking at herself, she felt young, maybe too young.

Backing away, she sighed, recognizing she still had a fair amount of time to kill. She spent it scrolling through social media posts of celebrities on the red carpet of some movie premiere from the night before, noticing plunging necklines must be "in" right now.

Violet decided not to get dressed until the last minute. She somehow thought that waiting would be better. If her outfit made her feel sexy, she didn't want to waste that energy sitting around her house alone. *Cosmo* always mentioned how clothes could totally transform you and give you more confidence, and she definitely would need it.

At 11:30, she approached her dresser and pulled open her underwear drawer. She didn't really have anything that seemed right for the occasion. She wondered why her underwear even mattered if they'd be coming off anyway.

Would they be coming off?

She remembered another article about the thrill of having sex with your clothes still on "just like when you were younger". Was she supposed to have sex with her clothes on the first time? That didn't seem right; how could holding your panties off to one side the whole time possibly be sexy?

She landed on a plain black thong. Incidentally, all she could think about was how this thong would now hold a wild memory by the end of the night. As of that moment, she had two major piles in her underwear drawer— period panties and the rest of them. Should there be a pile for sex undies? Was that normal?

She chose a plain black bra as well before layering a pair of jean shorts and a tank-top over them, and a headband to jazz up her ponytail a bit. Something still felt wrong.

She swapped out different pairs of earrings but couldn't figure out what was throwing her off when in reality she knew it had to be the nerves. She wondered if Emmy had spent this long assessing herself in the mirror before she lost her v-card. She couldn't imagine it, Emmy was just too confident, and she probably knew what she was doing, too.

The familiar buzz of her cell phone sounded from her nightstand, she picked it up immediately. Her stomach flipped as she noticed it was a message from Xander.

XANDER
You can come over whenever :)

It was 11:58.

Violet took a deep breath in and blew it out. It was go time.

She slipped her phone into her back pocket and quickly wandered down the stairs, grabbing her dad's keys from the rack near the garage door.

"Hey, I'm taking the car to go to lunch," she informed Mr. Gray, still set up on the couch, now watching some home improvement show.

He didn't look away, just gave a thumbs up to signal he had heard her and asked, "When will you be back?"

Violet hesitated. "Uh, a couple hours I guess." She felt that sting of lies and uncertainty on her tongue.

"Okay, sounds good."

Part of her hoped her dad would come up with a reason for her to stay. She stood another minute, waiting for at least a delay, but realized it wasn't coming and turned to get into her car.

At that moment, everything started to feel real. Was she really going through with this? Was it really going to happen?

In ten short minutes, she'd be knocking on Xander's door.

Would he make a move straight away? Would they just hang out like normal first? Her stomach started doing flips as she pulled up to a stoplight.

To her left sat a small Walgreen Pharmacy. And suddenly, she came to a realization.

Condoms.

She didn't have any, and she definitely wasn't on birth control. Should she stop?

No, that's a silly idea. She couldn't just roll into his house with a bag of condoms in hand, that's way too obvious.

But what if he didn't have any? Could she still go through with this?

She felt her stomach flipping at double speed as the light turned green.

No. She wouldn't stop. And if he didn't have condoms then it just wasn't meant to happen. That was the sign she'd wait for.

She pulled into his driveway. He lived in a corner house —it felt like every neighbor could see her car pulling in, though none of the neighbors were actually outside.

VIOLET
Hey, Im here!

Rather than exiting the car, she stared at the screen to see if he'd respond. For some reason, she kept imagining a message that said, "Never mind, go away."

Instead, the front door to the house opened, and Xander stood and waved at Violet, urging her to come inside.

Another deep breath and reassuring nod in the mirror later, she was inside, closing the door behind her.

"Hey!"

"Hey!"

An awkward silence followed.

"So, I was thinking we could watch a movie or something?" Xander offered.

Violet nodded casually. "Sure!"

She followed him into his living room and sat on the couch, intentionally leaving a good few inches or so between them.

"Have you seen *Sorority Slaughter* yet? My brother said he and his buddies watched it last weekend, and it was pretty good."

"I haven't seen it, no. I don't normally go for slasher flicks."

Xander hesitated. "Oh, you have something else you want to see, then?"

She thought a moment—what were the chances she'd see the whole movie anyway? Did it matter if this was just the alibi?

"You know what, let's watch it. If it came recommended, I'm sure it can't be that bad." She pulled her legs up to sit cross-legged on the couch as Xander smiled and clicked through the menu options to the movie.

"*Sorority Slaughter* it is, then," and he turned the lights down.

As the film began, it seemed like a usual college film, big parties and kids drinking straight from the kegs. It wasn't even four minutes before the screen was filled from left to right with a woman's breasts as she straddled a guy in a dark bedroom.

She blushed. Now she understood why Xander's brother and his friends liked the film so much.

She felt a movement and looked down slightly. She noticed Xander had inched a little closer, his hand rather close to resting on her knee.

She looked at him and smiled a little, also inching herself closer to him, resting her thigh on one, maybe two, of his fingers. One step at a time, she would get them closer. Focusing on the littlest motions of her body kept her from dwelling on the destination of this little journey. Xander slipped his fingers out from under her leg and rested his hand gently on her thigh, seeming to test his limits.

Violet made no reaction; this was just another step toward the goal. She played it cool; didn't say anything about it, just let it happen, slowly but surely moving her right shoulder closer to his left one. As strange as it felt to be closing the space between the two of them, she had her sights set on something more important.

Suffice it to say, Violet was focused so much on the subtle changes in the body language between them, she had totally stopped paying attention to the movie, and she had a slight suspicion that her friend had done the same.

Finally, she looked over her shoulder at him. He looked back. She took another tip from *Cosmo*, and instead of looking into his eyes, looked directly at his lips, hoping to send a simple yet clear message as to what was on her mind.

It must have worked, within moments of that look, their lips had pressed against each other, and Xander pushed hard against her, encouraging her to lay down.

She had kissed him before, of course, back when they had dated, but this time already felt insanely different. Her stomach circled around like a gymnast on the bars, jumping back and forth and up and down so much it felt unnatural.

Xander stopped and backed his head away from hers, looking down into her eyes. "Look, I know we're not together or anything, and if you're not cool with this, we can just finish the movie."

"No, it's fine. I know," Violet nodded to him, giving consent as hastily as she could manage. She didn't want to chicken out now. This would be a good thing for her; there had to be a reason she couldn't go a day without seeing sex everywhere. By the end of the afternoon, she would finally get it.

Xander still looked slightly hesitant as he nodded. "Okay." He paused and then said, "How far are you willing to go?"

Unsure of how to answer, Violet looked around the room, avoiding eye contact as she considered her response. She settled on, "Do you have any... you know... things?" She scrunched her nose as she said the final word, wondering why she took so long to respond with something that childish.

Xander squinted his eyes a bit, clearly confused by the ambiguous meaning of the word "things". *Stupid.* She began on a mental self-diatribe, ceasing only when the conversation continued.

"You mean, like...condoms?" He finally asked.

Violet nodded affirmatively. He already said it, she didn't need to repeat.

"Uh, yeah." He sat up. "Upstairs though," he spoke again, "If you'd like to come?" He smiled, though it seemed laced with nerves. Could he have possibly been more nervous than her?

He had the condoms. That was the sign she'd set for herself. Today would be the day.

So, she followed him up the stairs and into one of the many empty bedrooms. She exhaled one final, deep breath for preparation, and closed the door behind her.

CHAPTER FIVE

The ceiling laid bare, catching Violet's eye as it mocked the bodies below.

Though only a few moments had passed, time seemed exceptionally slow as Violet rushed to retrieve her clothes and Xander did the same.

She wasn't sure why it mattered if she dressed so quickly, Xander had already seen her, and touched her.

Did he touch her? It felt like a blur—it happened so quickly. It was basically an in-and-out situation lasting only a few minutes. They had kissed for a minute or two before fully disrobing. He rolled on a condom (not before flipping it over a few times to figure out which way was right) and thrust himself inside of her where they both laid in a relatively stillness until he removed himself less than a minute later, having completed his task.

The deed was done, and while Xander seemed positive, Violet felt—the same? She wondered if she was supposed to feel different.

"So…" Xander started, drawing Violet's attention to him as he sat on the corner of his bed, fully clothed again.

Violet played with the headband in her hair as she subtly avoided eye contact. It was fairly obvious neither of them knew what to say.

"I'm sorry," he said after a deep breath.

That caught Violet's full attention; she made a face of confusion. "What for?" she asked, full of concern.

Xander shrugged. "I don't know. I didn't last very long, and, I mean… this is awkward, right?"

Violet crossed her arms and sat on the opposite bed corner, watching her thumbs twiddle in her lap as she pondered what exactly to say next.

"I guess it's awkward, but everyone's first time is supposed to be awkward, I think." At least that's the impression she got from *Cosmo*.

That clearly had not been the right thing to say, as the disappointment radiating off Xander's body seemed to intensify. His shoulders slumped a little lower and his eyes aimed directly to the floor in front of him. Violet knew this was his first time too, and while he wouldn't admit it, she was certain he had to have felt just as nervous as she did.

She suddenly felt a little guilty. Shifting herself over to face her friend and putting on a genuine face, she said, "Xan, I'm glad we did this, awkward or not."

"Really?" His eyebrows raised suspiciously.

"Yes! I mean, when I was thinking about it, why not do it with a friend, you know? You're one of my closest friends and I trust you. Now we can't break up and regret it."

There was a pause, filled with uncertainty.

"We already did that," Violet added with a smile to lighten the mood. Xander also cracked a smile and a soft chuckle.

"Yeah, I guess you're right," he finally replied.

In the following silence, Violet reached into her pocket to grab her phone, suddenly unsure of what time it was. The clock reflected about one o'clock.

"Texting your friends about it already?" Xander's insecurity resurfaced, masking itself as a silly joke.

Violet gave him a playful side-eye. "No. I'm checking the time."

Xander nodded in understanding.

Another few moments of silence passed too slowly while the friends sat wondering what else they could possibly say. There was one more thing weighing on Violet's mind, but she just couldn't bring herself to ask it out loud.

"Well, I think I should go," Violet admitted. They both nodded, accepting that they probably needed some time to fully digest what had happened.

Xander stood and walked her to the front door. With one hand on the doorknob, he asked, "You sure you don't want to finish that movie?"

Violet laughed, "Yeah, I don't think that's my thing, but thanks."

Xander opened the door for her and offered a hug before she left. She gave him a brief hug before heading back out to her dad's car, tucking herself inside and buckling up, feeling a sort of ease. It was as if she'd been holding her breath in since she entered the house, and now she could breathe easy again, but despite this she wasn't completely relaxed. A new wave of anxiety had come.

Something felt different, but it just wasn't what she expected. She expected some sort of relief or excitement, but all she felt was… off, almost like something was missing.

She twisted the key in the ignition and slowly backed out of the driveway as Xander watched from his front door, disappearing back into his house as she switched the gear to drive forward on the street.

The events of that afternoon played back in her head. Now that Xander's eyes weren't on her, she found herself wanting to tell her friends. She was sitting on her phone, which resided in her back pocket. Looking at the clock again, she decided maybe going directly home now would be too early and her dad might be suspicious.

She hadn't eaten since that morning and decided impulsively to turn into a local sub shop to eat and kill some more time before heading home.

The store was empty, save for one elderly gentleman, eating what appeared to be a meatball sub at the very back table. He didn't even look up when the bell jingled, signaling the employees that someone had come into the shop.

"Hi! What can I get for you?" a polite employee asked. She was about Violet's age, maybe a bit older.

Violet smiled and requested a turkey sub. As she moved along the production line, watching her sandwich being built, she couldn't help but wonder; did she look different? Was she acting differently? Could this employee tell she was not a virgin just at first glance?

People talked about pregnancy glow, but was there a sex glow she didn't know about? Would her dad be able to tell when she got home?

Violet assessed the employee as she wrapped her sandwich up. *How can you tell just by looking at someone if they've had sex?* She couldn't discern whether she had, so maybe Violet was safe too.

She paid with a few singles in her wallet and sat down at a central table, looking out at the parking lot. She gathered up some nerve, pulling her phone from her pocket and setting it beside her sandwich on the table, began drafting a message to Xander.

Now she had the time to really choose her words and phrases exactly as she wanted to. She'd be able to ask him:

VIOLET

Be honest. Did you expect all that to happen today?

Something still felt wrong about actually saying the word "sex". She'd subconsciously resolved to only use euphemisms for the time being, and she had a good arsenal of them stocked up in her vocabulary. Practically anything could be used to signify sex these days. She felt lucky that was the case.

XANDER
No. I just kinda hoped it would.

VIOLET

Just wanted to get it over with?

XANDER
Maybe a little.
I wasnt sure you were going to be into it though.

Kinda surprised it happened so fast

lol

VIOLET

I mean, you invited me over with no

parents. Thats kind of a universal

signal.

XANDER

Made it too obvious then? lol

Violet sighed, reading through the messages. It wasn't obvious to her, it took Jess pointing it out for her to even realize Xander was putting out signals. She knew they weren't going to get back together. They've discussed that idea for what felt like one-hundred times; a close friendship just worked better for them was always the consensus. The idea of them as a romantic couple only came up so often because they were so close, people tended to assume. She hoped what they'd done wouldn't change anything for them.

VIOLET

Maybe. You still don't want to get

back together right?

XANDER

Nah it'd be weird.

VIOLET

Weirder than this? Lol

Violet took a large bite out of her sandwich and chewed, staring at her phone screen as the "Typing…" notification sat at the bottom of her messaging app.

XANDER
Lol. You going to tell anyone?

VIOLET

Do you not want me to?

XANDER
I guess it doesn't matter

VIOLET

You gonna tell Trav?

He didn't respond immediately. He didn't even start typing.

Violet's eyes narrowed as she swallowed one of the final bites of her turkey sandwich, wondering if it was possible that Travis encouraged Xander to try this with her in the first place.

She imagined Xander engaging in the locker room talk and telling other guys about her body or making fun of how awkward she was. Or telling people it was her idea to go upstairs when Xander asked how far she'd go.

She stopped that train of thought before it got too far and was eased a little by Xander's response.

XANDER
Do you not want me to?

He hit her back with the same words she'd asked him, but she felt a little more confident knowing Xander would keep this secret between them if she wanted. He was a good friend, that's why she did this in the first place.

She took another second to think about her potential response. Travis was sort of a "bro" type, but she'd known Xander for years now—he wouldn't talk about her like that. She trusted him, that's why she was willing to do any of this in the first place.

VIOLET
Its fine. Lets just not make a big
thing out of it.

XANDER
Deal :)

This was good. This was okay. She could handle everything with Xander, she would tell her friends, and she didn't have to be Virgin Violet anymore. She could confidently move on, and not have to worry about what her first time would be like because it was already done.

Still, even with all the potential drama settled in her mind, her stomach felt knotted and surprisingly heavy.

The words "first time" rung in her ears. Would there be a second? A third? And would she do it with Xander? Should she wait until she was in a relationship? All these questions raced through her head, repeating themselves over and over again as she swallowed the final piece of her sandwich and she stared at the empty tray in front of her. She was the one all of her friends went to when they needed advice, it wasn't often she was the one needing the advice. At this moment, she could feel a strange and lonely reality in that even now that she'd had sex, her experience was so different it was almost like she hadn't done it at all. She wanted to be able to relate to her peers more, but she couldn't feel further apart. In hindsight, Virgin Violet didn't seem so bad.

It was only one-thirty, but it felt so much later. It felt like so much had transpired in the last hour and a half. It seemed as though it should be dark out by now, but the sun still hung overhead, like a bright, yellow, all-seeing eye.

She threw away her wrapper and set the tray on top of the trashcan as she headed out the door, feeling the eye's heat on her back as she ducked into her car once more. Finally ready to return home, with the loose ends tied and questions answered with Xander, still one question burned at the back of her head, even hotter than the sun's glare.

What was so great about it?

CHAPTER SIX

As Violet drove home, she recalled the time Emmy announced to her and Yvonne that she was "now a woman."

EMMY
It happened!

VIOLET
What did?

EMMY
I'm a woman now ;)

VIOLET
What do you mean?

EMMY
I'll tell you tomorrow.

Violet couldn't even imagine just sending a text like that to her friends, and especially with as many details as Emmy would likely request.

She had received that text from Emmy several months prior, and that Monday when they came into school, she practically steamrolled over her friends as they sat outside the cafeteria, waiting for the first bell to ring and the day to begin.

She had stood tall with a certain air of confidence about her that only appeared slightly more aggressive than usual. "Well, do I look different?" she asked, turning to show herself at every angle.

Yvonne and Violet only exchanged a glance and a surprised smile.

"Yeah, we hardly recognized you," Violet spoke sarcastically.

Emmy narrowed her eyes and crossed her arms. "Oh, come on. You're not even going to ask me about it?"

Yvonne let out a laugh and responded, "Okay, tell us about it. Who was it?"

Emmy perked up and leaned into her two friends so they might recognize the secretive nature of what she was about to say. "Do you remember that super hot guy we saw at the carnival a few weeks ago?"

Violet certainly remembered Emmy freaking out and making googly eyes at someone between bites of a significantly oversized funnel cake.

She nodded anyway. "Yeah."

"Well, it turns out he goes to our church. So my mom was having some coffee and kissing up to the pastor or whatever, and I see him standing all alone in the corner eating this chocolate muffin, so I go over to him, and I started talking to him about how he managed to get one because, like, they're always the first to go, and he's like 'You just gotta be faster,' and he was totally giving me these eyes, right? So I was like, complaining about how I'd probably be there for another hour because my mom was feeling chatty, and he said his parents always stay really late too and asked if I wanted to take a walk around the building or something. Obviously I said yes, and we went out and walked around the parking lot, and we're talking and everything, and we get to the back of the church right by all those trees, and I just stopped walking, and I was leaning all casually up against this tree, right? And I'm putting off the craziest signals—like, full-on chest puffed, wide-eyed looking up at him so he'd get the hint, and he totally went for it! We started making out and he had his hands *alllll* over me," she said this, rubbing her hands up and down on her upper arms.

"And he kinda like, pulled my dress up with his finger and just…" she groaned in excitement. "It was incredible. He held me up against the tree and, *damn*, he knows how to treat a lady right. I was basically walking like a baby giraffe back into the church to find my mom."

"And she didn't notice?" Violet wondered.

"I snapped out of it real fast, because get this," she got in close again, "The guy is the pastor's *son*!"

Yvonne and Violet's jaws simultaneously dropped to the floor as they murmured their disbelief.

"Yeah! It was like some movie-level plot twist, for sure."

"For sure." Yvonne nodded, somehow with disbelief in her eyes.

"You gonna see him again?" Violet inquired.

"That's the thing, we were kind of busy the whole time, I didn't really get his number. Maybe I'll ask him next week, you know, if we don't get too busy again," she said, smiling suggestively.

As Violet recalled, they did end up exchanging numbers and sending flirty texts to each other, if salacious photos could fit into that category, but nothing else became of it. Soon enough they were talking less and less frequently and he just disappeared from Emmy's daily updates as she focused her attention on new men of interest.

So Emmy had this amazing story to share, Yvonne would have weeks of meet-cutes leading up to the romantic loss of her flower, and Violet had… this.

Suddenly she felt self-conscious, what would she even say? "I decided to have sex this weekend?"

She glanced down at her knees; she didn't recall them wobbling like a baby giraffe as she followed Xander down the staircase. Was that wrong? Were they supposed to be wobbling? Did she overthink it so much she couldn't enjoy it?

Emmy said her first time was incredible, but how would Violet describe hers? She thought carefully about the events.

She pulled the car up through the driveway and into the garage. It somehow appeared more chaotic and messy than it had the day before. Maybe there was more junk piled up, but she didn't notice anything new.

She sat with the car idling for a few moments, building a list in her head of what she might say when she finally gave her big announcement.

- Brief
- Uncomfortable
- Nerve-racking

She made a face as she twisted the key out of her car's ignition.

- Fine

It wasn't the worst thing she'd ever done, but it definitely wasn't "incredible". She wasn't dying to do it again as Emmy led her to believe she would.

Maybe it was just that she and Xander were both new to this. Maybe they missed some of the steps? Should she have waited to experience her first time with someone who knew what they were doing? Would that make more sense?

No. She couldn't imagine doing that. She didn't want to lose her virginity to someone random who she'd never see or talk to again; that's why she decided to go through with this in the first place.

She entered her home and closed the garage door behind her. It looked as though her dad was in the bathroom. That could be awhile.

Her fingers dropped the keys onto the counter and she quickly hustled upstairs, sitting herself down at her desk and hastily raising the screen to her laptop.

It didn't power up fast enough for her. She impatiently tapped her fingers as the log-in screen took its time to reveal itself. She typed her password and unlocked an internet window which she'd left up from a few nights ago, listing formulas she had needed for her chemistry homework.

It disappeared rather quickly as she clicked into the address bar and navigated to her go-to source of information, *Cosmopolitan.*

She scanned the screen for a search bar and typed inside the box, "first time", hesitating only a moment before swiftly tapping the "enter" key on her keyboard, yielding a list of results and articles she could preview before deciding which would be most helpful.

She clicked on one. It was exactly what she'd been looking for: "11 Girls Reveal What They Wish They Had Known Before Having Sex for the First Time."

It was obviously a little late for this, but maybe it would help her understand what went so wrong. Was it guilt, or first-time jitters? Something about it just felt wrong and she needed to know why that was.

She scanned the article, reading miniature headlines about pain, making sure it's the right person, being comfortable, and being fun. Was it fun?

What stood out the most to her was the section about orgasms.

That had to be it—she didn't have an orgasm! It was weird and uncomfortable for her because he was able to finish and she didn't. That made the most sense. They'd never done this before, he probably didn't know what he had to do for everything to go right, and she didn't really have any idea as to what would help her feel satisfied.

Nothing was wrong, they're just inexperienced.

She dove into the rabbit hole of other articles—"The 8 Best First-Time Sex Positions", "11 Sex Positions that will Help You Orgasm, Guaranteed." She read other women's stories about their first times. She studied images and took mental notes.

Why hadn't she done this before? The more she read, the more everything made sense to her. It would get better with practice. The reason Emmy's first time must have been so good for her was because the pastor's son really knew what he was doing (which gave her a little ironic giggle).

She absorbed the information like a dehydrated sponge. "What Guys Most Want From You In Bed", "20 Fun Ways to Spice Things Up Under the Sheets". She scrolled through mentions of whipped cream, and toys, where to put your hands, fancy scented candles, and sensual massages.

Before long, it was decided in her mind; she would have to have sex again, and it would most certainly be better than the first time. How could it not be with all the interesting new techniques she had learned?

She found herself finally understanding why Elle Woods had called this magazine "the Bible".

A knock came at her bedroom door. She tapped incessantly at the "x" at the top corner of her screen until the window disappeared, displaying her desktop screen loaded with pictures of herself and her friends.

Mr. Gray opened the door and smiled. "Hey, Vi, I got something to run by ya."

"Okay," Violet said, hoping her urgency and residual fear in her voice from almost being caught wouldn't give too much away.

Her father gave no indication to noticing anything different. He sat on the edge of her bed while she remained in her desk chair.

"I was thinking, you've had your license for a while and you have yet to crash the old Chevy," he pointed out the window with his thumb, not really anywhere near where the car sat in the garage. "So maybe it might be a good idea to talk about you getting one of your own. My bud Jerry has a used car lot downtown, so we might be able to get you a good deal."

Violet smiled and nodded. "Yeah, that would be awesome!"

At that moment, she wasn't sure what excited her more: the prospect of getting her very own car, or the fact that her dad seemed blissfully unaware that something in his daughter had changed that afternoon.

"Great! We can pull up his website and look through what he's got after dinner, sounds good?" he asked, patting his legs and standing up.

"You bet."

With those words, Mr. Gray exited through the doorway, leaving Violet to sit alone, once again, with her computer so she could continue her fall down the rabbit hole.

CHAPTER SEVEN

Birds chirped outside the window as Violet laid in her bed that Monday morning. How odd, she didn't normally hear them that early. She hadn't slept the best. She'd spent her spare time over the weekend sitting at her computer, doing a little more research in some incognito tabs, and trying to think of the best way to tell her friends what she'd done that weekend.

Yvonne didn't respond much in their group chats that weekend, and as Violet attempted to withhold her big secret until she saw her friends in person, the chat was just a constant string of texts from Emmy.

EMMY
Any juicy updates, Y?
… busy I see.

I'm so booorrrrreeedddd.

Violet opened her eyes, glaring at the sliver of sunlight breaking its way into her bedroom from behind the curtain.

Then it hit her. She sat up quickly, pulling her phone off the nightstand beside her to look at the time.

Seven o'clock.

The first bell sounded at 7:15 am.

She kicked her duvet off her legs and rushed into her dad's room.

"Dad! I'm late, get up!" She shook him by the shoulders until he gasped and sat up straight.

"What?"

"I overslept. It's 7 o'clock, I need you to take me to school," she said, trying her hardest to express a sense of urgency to her groggy father.

He nodded with one fist rubbing the tiredness from his eyes. "Okay, okay. Go get dressed. I'll go start the car."

Violet rushed to get herself ready, pulling a pair of "school appropriate" jeans over her hips as she stacked her homework, still resting on the corner of her desk, haphazardly in her backpack.

The stairs creaked loudly as she stumbled down them into the kitchen where she grabbed a granola bar out of the cabinet to eat on the way, and she checked her wallet to see if she had enough cash to pay for a school lunch. Everything seemed in order.

Mr. Gray was still waking up as he opened up the garage door and sat himself in the driver's seat, looking like a zombie compared to the frazzled teenager beside him.

He started the car and pulled out slowly. It was 7:15 now, and Violet would surely be late.

She chewed her granola bar while she dabbed some concealer under her eyes and put on some mascara in the tiny visor mirror.

"What happened?" her father asked, punctuating his question with a yawn.

"I don't know, I guess I forgot to set my alarm before I fell asleep."

He accepted this response, keeping his eyes on the road ahead, though mumbling quietly about how he couldn't wait until she had her own car.

He pulled up to the front of the school building at about 7:25 am; Violet hardly managed to wait for the car to stop moving before pushing the door open.

"Thanks, Dad!" she called, slamming the door closed behind her and fast walking her way up to the main entrance. She'd have to collect her tardy slip before heading to her math class.

The secretary rolled her eyes as she filled the slip with the phrase "overslept". It seemed that was a popular excuse for the day, based on the handful of students lined up with Violet for the same reason. She collected her slip and was finally able to head to class a little after 7:30. Now that she had a pass, she was able to relax a little and made her way to class at a more normal pace.

The halls were mostly empty. She passed some classrooms with open doors and teachers lecturing desks full of half-asleep students.

She glanced at her phone and took notice of a few texts from her friends.

YVONNE
Where are you?
EMMY
Ditching today?

She sighed, slipping her phone into the front pocket of her bag as she approached her classroom. The door was closed, of course.

She knocked on the door and waited for her teacher to open it. She handed him her pink slip and he motioned for her to take her seat.

Violet found her seat, ignoring the judging eyes of other students all on her and pulling her notebooks and pencils from her backpack. Travis sat in the seat diagonal from her to the front and left, Xander sat on the other side of the classroom. Violet had yet to look in his direction, though she wasn't certain why.

Travis turned and leaned over her desk, whispering, "I really thought you were ditching."

"Why?" Violet creased her forehead in confusion.

"I don't know," he shrugged, "but I got a *lot* of questions about what happened this weekend." He gave a mischievous smirk and turned back around.

Violet could feel herself blushing a little. She didn't think she'd feel this embarrassed.

All anyone ever talking about at this school was "body counts" and how their parents caught them. The varsity quarterback was busted for sleeping with half the JV cheerleaders, so why did it have to be a big deal what she did over the weekend with a close friend?

She copied down the information that was written on the board before she got into class, trying her best to catch up, but in the back of her mind, she kept telling herself she needed to be more casual and relax a little. She felt so on edge. The only way this would be a big deal was if she made it a big deal.

The teacher droned on as he began to take a backseat to the rampant thoughts in Violet's mind. For about the hundredth time since that morning, she began wondering if she'd made a mistake. Losing her virginity to a friend seemed like a good idea, but what if it just made her seem like a slut? Is that what Travis thought?

But then again, why did she care what Travis thought? He was what she and the majority of her friends described as the "Chad type". He cared too much about being athletic and getting girls. He humble bragged a whole lot and generally just liked to feel like he was above everyone else. Violet knew he wasn't, so his opinion really shouldn't matter to her.

Her notebook page was filled with formulas that didn't make sense. She scanned through the symbols, trying to make sense of them before she heard the teacher speaking.

"Alright, the last ten minutes will be work time. On page 413, I want you to do all the even numbers through question 30. You can work with whoever you want."

Violet rose to head to the bookshelf housing all the textbooks and lined up with other students to grab them, as she returned to her seat, Xander had taken a seat beside Travis, and the two of them had angled themselves to include Violet in their work session.

This was not unusual. This was normally how their work time went in this class, but somehow, today, it felt like Violet had the two of them ganging up on her. She offered a slight, disingenuous smile as she sat and began flipping to page 413.

"Fifteen questions aren't so bad," Xander offered   to   break   the   uncomfortable   silence developing as Travis eyed Violet expectantly and she actively avoided eye contact.

"Speaking of not so bad," Travis took the opportunity, "Violet, how was it?" He used his elbow to nudge her forearm slightly.

She glanced up from the textbook and rolled her eyes at Travis, "Thank you for your interest, but I don't think it's any of your business." She spoke with the cadence of a customer service representative dismissing a customer with an expired coupon.

"Ouch," he winced as if he'd just been punched, and returned with, "That bad, huh?"

Xander narrowed his eyes, "Shut up, dude."

"Oh, come on! You're really gonna leave me in the dark here? I can't just wait around for gym for the locker room talk." He laughed at his own joke.

A few curious ears perked up, listening to the comments Travis made, perhaps a bit too loudly.

"It's not a big deal. We did it, and it's done," Violet shrugged, looking Xander in the eye for the first time since their weekend adventure, "Right?"

Xander nodded. "Right. Let's just leave it alone." He turned his attention back to the book.

"So, what? You're not getting back together or anything?" Travis spoke skeptically.

"Nope," Violet replied matter-of-factly.

"Damn, Xan. Your first time was a one-night stand. How's that make you feel?" He continued to try and push their buttons.

Xander rolled his eyes and kept his attention on his paper. "So, did you do anything fun yesterday?" He attempted to redirect the conversation to something a bit more mundane and casual.

"Or anyone?" Travis hissed in laughter under his breath.

Violet and Xander ignored him. "Yeah, actually. I started looking at some used cars with my dad on Saturday."

"Really?"

"Yeah, I guess he's tired of waking up early to drive me to school when I oversleep," she smiled, enjoying this far more comfortable conversation, though short-lived as it was going to be.

"Make sure you get one with seats that go *alllll* the way down. You can't keep relying on parents going out of town to get laid," Travis added, scribbling out the answer to the first math problem on his wrinkled paper.

"That's actually at the top of my list for consideration," Violet retorted, her words absolutely soaking in sarcasm. She was convinced if she rolled her eyes any harder, they would get stuck in the back of her head.

"It was for me. Slide that passenger seat all the way back, drop it all the way down and you got a bedroom of wheels." His smile was not subtle, nor were the implications.

Xander made a face. "For real, man?"

"Aw, relax. We keep it clean," Travis insisted.

Violet made a gagging noise and Travis found himself laughing at her general discomfort for the remainder of the class period.

Once the bell released them to the halls to make their way to their next class, Xander made an awkward point of bidding Violet farewell as they went their separate ways while Travis watched and drank in every possible ounce of awkwardness, likely to use it against Xander later in the day.

The halls filled quickly as Violet dodged the bodies of her peers in an effort to make it on time to her next class at least while her classmates spread the news.

Violet Gray had slept with Xander Dawes this past weekend while his parents were out of town, and even when her peers filtered into their respective classrooms, the whispers stayed, lingering in the walls.

CHAPTER EIGHT

The ring of the lunch bell bounced off Violet's eardrum hard. She'd spent so much of the first half of her day listening so closely to the whispers of her peers that the high-pitched chirp felt like a personal attack—karma getting back at her for being so nosy about what others were talking about.

She couldn't help it though.

All day it had felt as though Violet could hear her name everywhere she went. Even strangers at her huge school with a population of two thousand seemed to pay her an unexpected amount of attention. She couldn't help but wonder if it was all in her head as she entered the lunch line and collected the most edible-looking food from the long metallic buffet.

She felt the burning sensation of someone watching her and glanced at the student behind her through her peripherals. Was he looking at her?

She fully turned her head and his eyes were on a surprisingly straight banana he pulled from the pile of far limper and less appetizing fruits along their path.

Her lips angled to one side, somewhat frustrated with her own apparent paranoia that people somehow *knew* she was no longer a virgin and that's why she kept hearing her name or thinking people were looking at her.

The woman cashing out her lunch swiped her Student ID card and returned it to her with the same old smile and well-wish for a great day. It felt so comforting yet so out of place to move through a typical routine and engage in this very normal interaction. Even her footsteps felt off like her hips swayed just a bit more on their way to her usual table by the water fountain, where Yvonne sat waiting with her familiar boxed lunch: a turkey sandwich, baby carrots, and a bag of pretzel sticks.

Yvonne raised a small, orange nugget to her mouth and crunched, watching Violet walk to her like everyone else.

Violet set her tray down and pulled out a blue plastic chair, same as every day— but today it wasn't the same.

"Hey," she spoke casually, resting herself in the seat and smiling.

"Hey, where were you this morning?" Yvonne countered; her eyes filled with genuine curiosity.

"I slept in. Dad had to drive me to school," she spoke quickly before taking her first bite into a bland, yet perfectly rounded scoop of mashed potatoes.

"Oh" was Yvonne's only response.

The silence lasted a bit too long.

"How was your weekend?" Violet asked, her paranoia rising.

"Fine," Yvonne nodded, "Nothing exciting." Was she avoiding eye contact?

Buzz buzz.

A text message made its arrival known in the back pocket of Violet's jeans.

EMMY
Is it true?

Violet stopped for a moment and really looked at the text. Yvonne suddenly couldn't keep her eyes off her.

Maybe Violet wasn't so paranoid after all.

VIOLET
Is what true

EMMY
You and Xander

Violet stared at those words harder than the many sets of eyes staring at her now.

She was right, everyone did know. She suddenly thought back to how loud Travis had laughed during first period, she replayed the snickers as she passed some random guys in the hallway, and the side-eye she received from a girl she was now certain was in the celibacy club at a local church.

Violet radiated anxiety. Her cheeks flushed red in anger or maybe embarrassment, she wasn't completely sure.

Her eyes moved to Yvonne who appeared to be sucking the salt off of a single pretzel stick.

"How many people do you think have heard?" She didn't feel the need to confess, she was fairly certain Yvonne had known.

"I don't think everyone. Some people don't care about that stuff, you know?"

This didn't help Violet feel better, she set her phone down and just looked across the table, afraid of making any motions to indicate shame to this audience around her. She twiddled her thumbs on the table and bit her lower lip, considering how this jury of her peers was judging her now. She didn't just lose her virginity, she lost it to an ex-boyfriend. What implications did that have? That she's desperate? A slut? She felt all the confidence in her decision fading away and turning into something unexpected: fear.

What if this got back to her dad? What if her teachers knew? What if someone wrote her phone number next to a urinal in the bathroom indicating they should call her for a good time? She briefly considered sneaking into the boy's room to check before Yvonne snapped her out of her trance.

"It's kind of funny, isn't it?"

Violet looked up. "What do you mean?"

"I mean, at the end of last week, all the talk was that I'd be the one taking the plunge this weekend," she offered lightheartedly. "And now I'm the only virgin in the group."

Violet recalled a crude joke Emmy had made about how Steven would be the one doing all the plunging but chose to circumvent the thought when she realized what Yvonne was trying to say.

"You didn't do it?" Her shock was evident.

Yvonne shook her head with her eyebrows raised, waiting for the reaction to what had now become her confession.

Violet's thoughts went spinning rampantly again. She felt all the possible regrets, ideas, and fears battling together in her brain like it was WrestleMania with the walls of her skull acting like the cage, keeping the thoughts from exiting until only one remained.

Did she rush to lose her virginity for nothing?

"What happened?" She pushed Yvonne to speak more, afraid of what she might spill from her lips if the topic didn't stay on the tale of Steven and the great mystery of the intact hymen.

She sort of shrugged. "I don't really know, I guess I just couldn't go through with it. We were in the woods; we found a little field. We were watching the stars, and we started kissing…" she looked off toward the window, "But when the time came and he asked if I wanted to go any further, I just said no. We just kind of cuddled and talked for the rest of the night, it was actually really nice."

Violet could tell Yvonne was being honest. She had a hint of wistfulness in her eyes as if she was daydreaming of being back in that field again.

Now the memories of those few minutes in Xander's bedroom flooded back chronologically, playing like a movie beside the scene Yvonne described. She could hear the hypothetical moviegoers in her ears screaming at the girl in the darkened room and urging her to go sit under the stars instead. If only it were that easy.

"Anyway," Yvonne's voice once again brought her back to the white noise of the cafeteria. "Did you want to talk about what happened?"

Violet's nose scrunched up and she exhaled slowly through her mouth.

"I don't regret it," were the first thoughts to manifest themselves into the air. They flitted away quickly; she had to keep going, "I was thinking about it all weekend and I thought I'd rather get it over with and sleep with a good friend so I wouldn't get my heart broken by some random douche in college and I wouldn't have to deal with Emmy pestering me about when I'd do it." Though she attempted to deliver this information with a logical and matter-of-fact tone, it did have something of an edge that stung Yvonne. It felt oddly reminiscent of defensiveness.

Yvonne didn't have an immediate response.

"Now I don't have to freak out about my first time," she decided that was a better ending to her manifesto. "No more Virgin Violet," she chuckled at her own private joke.

Yvonne nodded. "I guess now we just have to worry about Virgin Yvonne."

Violet's face soured at the sadness of the idea. She had gone through this whole ordeal to avoid that title. Yvonne donning it so easily seemed so depressing and self-deprecating.

Yvonne sensed this from her old friend. "It's fine, Vi. I've been dealing with Emmy talking about my potential sexual escapades for weeks now. I knew this would happen when I said no to Steven. Honestly, it doesn't bother me at all. I'm immune." She lightly tapped her chest to signify its strength.

Violet wished she could have accepted her faith with as much dignity, but there was no turning back now. She had become someone new: Valiant Violet, or Vivacious, perhaps, would be more appropriate.

"But I have to ask," Yvonne began again, "I'm gathering you and Xander aren't planning on getting back together, right?"

Violet nodded with a question resting upon her brow. "Right…"

"So," Yvonne attempted to fill this space with rotating hands of hesitancy, "Are you friends with benefits or what?"

The question sat for a moment while it sank into Violet and to Yvonne's surprise, she began laughing.

Between giggles, she started, "No, no. I mean," she broke to cough out a few more laughs, "It was both of our first times and honestly, I've been thinking about doing it again. It was just a little strange and awkward when we did it." She made sure those words only made it to Yvonne's ears and not those of the passing noses attempting to rest themselves in her business.

"How so?" Yvonne inquired.

"It was just quick... and weird."

"Did it hurt?"

"No! It just wasn't," she searched for the right word, "Good, I guess."

Yvonne nodded in a somewhat confused understanding. Much like Violet, she'd been predisposed to think sex was always amazing (or at least it always was for Emmy).

"But that's normal. The first time isn't always supposed to be good. I just think with a little more foreplay and if I just guided him a little more, then it would be great."

Violet felt so correct and intelligent as she recited what she'd learned from her deep dive into *Cosmo* that weekend.

Her confidence was slowly returning.

Though she didn't have all the experience, she definitely felt more prepared, and as she faked her certainty that sex the second time would be incomparably better than the first, her shoulders rolled back, and she held her head a little higher.

"So, you *are* gonna do it again," Yvonne clarified, "with Xander, I mean?"

"Yeah, I mean, if he wants to," she began wondering aloud before catching her confidence faltering again. She added, "I'm sure he does. What guy doesn't?"

Her fingers pushed the lock screen away from her as she navigated through her apps to land on her messages again. She was met with Emmy's last message again and decided to ignore it and let her twist in the wind a little longer.

She swiped her way through her recent conversations, stopping on Xander's name and hitting the "+" button to compose her new message.

VIOLET
FYI, I do think the seats in my new
car will go all the way down

CHAPTER NINE

Violet scrolled through her texts from the day as she wandered through the halls to her last class, the same one in which she'd finally see Emmy for the first time that day.

XANDER
Really? lol

VIOLET
Yeah, it's a hatchback :)

XANDER
So you want to hang out soon?

VIOLET
And do what?

XANDER
I have some ideas…

VIOLET
Your parents still out of town?

XANDER
Nah, but maybe we could meet up
after school or something and take a
walk out by the baseball fields

VIOLET
Today?

XANDER
Or whenever

VIOLET
I'll let you know

;)

She was uncertain as to what was keeping her anxiety at an all-time high: the fact that she was so obviously making herself available to her ex-boyfriend, or the certainty of the law-enforcement quality interview she would be receiving from Emmy during this period.

"Violet!" Emmy sang from across the room, sitting atop a lab table, waving to catch her friend's attention as quickly as possible.

Yeah, this was definitely the greater source of anxiety.

Violet casually approached the table and set her things down, beginning to unpack her chemistry homework from her bag to avoid the pleading eyes of a gossip-starved teenage girl.

"I know you saw my text, missy! Start talking," Emmy demanded, absolutely glowing with anticipation.

"I did," Violet played coy, "And it's not a big deal. Plus class is starting in two minutes." Her heart pounded against her chest as she attempted to avoid the conversation.

"Please," Emmy's eyes rolled. The two girls hardly noticed that Yvonne had joined them at their table. "I can get a ton of information in two minutes."

"Well, a minute and a half now," Violet pointed out.

Yvonne was already smiling. Violet wondered if maybe she was enjoying not being the object of Emmy's peer-pressure more than she'd let on at lunch.

"Look, there is conflicting information out there! Someone said you did it in his parent's bed. Did you?" she pried.

"Really?"

"I heard that too, but I also heard you snuck into his window last night after his parents got home and that's why you overslept this morning."

Violet decided against telling them the real reason was that she forgot to set her alarm while reading an opinion piece in *Cosmo* about why anal play should be a part of every foreplay routine (though she did not share this sentiment).

"That's just talk," she waved the ideas away. "It was totally normal, nothing weird or wild like that."

The bell rang.

"Alright, class," the chemistry teacher, Ms. Elliot, announced, collecting the student's attention rather immediately.

Emmy hopped off the table in a huff and gave her friend a whiny side-eyed glance as she sat herself in a chair.

As the class began, and students opened up their notebooks to start drawing out the equations Ms. Elliot displayed on the board, Violet noticed Emmy taking better notes than usual. She was hunched over her notebook, scribbling out words and appeared to be making some sort of table. She ripped it out of her spiral-bound book (leaving the ragged edges attached), folded it in half and slid it across the table so it got one corner stuck under Violet's notebook.

Violet stared at it for a second, glanced over to Emmy who now had focused on writing the equations she had apparently not even started on, and finally looked to Ms. Elliot who was conveniently not looking at their table.

Once open, Violet noticed a crudely drawn ruler over the crease from her fold, with two words scribbled in Emmy's horrible handwriting across the header.

how big?

Violet crumpled up the sheet and dropped it into her open backpack beside her chair. She was satisfied with the visual of her navy JanSport swallowing the wad of paper where it now rested, unlikely to be seen again until her yearly bag clean-out right before the next school year started.

She maintained attention on the board, ignoring Emmy as Ms. Elliot queued up a video of animated blobs that would explain the equations they had just written down.

Idle chatter broke out as it normally did whenever their teacher provided even a moment of down-time. She could feel Emmy leaning closer to her from her chair at the end of the table beside her.

"How many times did you do it?" She whispered to not trigger any wrath from Ms. Elliot, still in technology troubleshooting mode.

Violet didn't answer.

"Okay, okay," she attempted to negotiate her prioritized details out of Violet, "Just tell me this: was it good?"

That was the one question, of course, that Violet didn't want to answer. There was no way to word it that seemed fair to Xander or herself. The fact that she really didn't enjoy her first time wasn't really anyone's fault, but it could certainly sound that way. She considered all of her possible responses:

- "Yeah," a lie, and
- "No," the truth.

Of course, in the back of her mind, she had her third option, the more accurate truth:

- "Not yet"

Fake It till You Make It

It would get better. It happened for tons of women who wrote to *Cosmo*, it changed the lives of every teenager in every YA book she'd ever read, and it felt like the number one defining characteristic of students at this school. A game of *Truth or Dare* just wasn't complete without the classics: "Are you a virgin?" and "How many people have you had sex with?"

Somehow the question would have been better if Emmy had asked, "How was it?" instead of, "Was it good?"

Just because she didn't think it was good didn't mean she thought it was necessarily "bad". It just... was.

Once again, Violet was saved by Ms. Elliot redirecting the class's attention, imploring the students to quiet down and pay attention to the clip she was playing on the screen.

Violet watched as the electrons of a hydrogen molecule ran laps around the nucleus. If only she could run from this conversation.

Emmy sulked the remainder of the lesson as Violet ignored her incessant, (albeit creative) questioning, but perked up at the mention of work-time.

Violet grew frustrated, suddenly displeased that her teachers didn't do bell-to-bell lectures.

Emmy slammed her notebook shut and plopped her elbows on the table, giving Violet an expectant look over the tops of her cat-eye glasses.

Violet's right heel bounced up and down under the table in perfect time with her pencil's eraser tapping against the textbook before her.

"It's time, Vi. You gotta give me something." Her words felt calm and direct. Emmy was her friend, and she should be able to trust her with her secrets.

"We watched a movie together and it just happened—in his room, not his parents. Then I left. It was totally normal and," she stopped herself from saying unexciting. That phrasing seemed to carry some negative implications so she decided on "usual. Exactly what you'd expect."

"That's it?" Emmy pressed, not quite believing that was all to the tale.

"Yup, perfectly typical."

"And his dick?"

"Emmy…" Yvonne inserted herself into the conversation.

"Normal," Violet offered in an attempt to ease her curiosity.

"Alright, Goldilocks," Emmy said, turning her unsatisfied face to the work she'd been putting off.

Violet and Yvonne exchanged a confused look before Emmy tacked on an explanation. "Not too big, not too small. Just right." There was a pause, "I guess you're the only one left, Yvonne," she spoke with a large smile adorning her face.

A knock came at the door. A student nearby jumped at the opportunity to get out of his desk and opened the door.

It was Jess.

The whole class had looked up at the first hint of something or someone interesting being at the door but quickly returned to their work. Violet, however, watched as Jess approached Ms. Elliot's desk. She tossed a quick glance and polite smile at Violet as she passed her and before resting some papers on Ms. Elliot's desk and beginning a quiet conversation that Violet couldn't make out.

She wondered if Jess had heard the news. She felt her confidence waning. Explaining the situation to Jess after she'd made such a big deal about not wanting to lose her v-card any time soon felt like answering to a parent. She fully expected the use of the, "I'm not mad; I'm just disappointed" line.

Violet and her tablemates wrapped up their work and began filing their work into their backpacks, initiating the first few notes in the zipper chorus signifying the few minutes remaining in class.

Jess still spoke with Ms. Elliot, though they seemed happy and friendly. She provided a final, "Thank you!" before exiting to the hallway, but not without a detour at Violet's table by the window.

"You still need a ride home today?" she inquired, appearing far too relaxed and collected. It reminded her of the time she copped an attitude with her grandmother after she got reprimanded for being "on her phone all the time." Her mother immediately and politely asked Violet to go into the next room with her before completely blowing up.

"Yeah," she answered simply.

"Great. We can walk to my car together."

CHAPTER TEN

The shout of the end-of-the-day bell seemed to echo against her ears from a distance, contrasting its usual screech. Although Violet had strategically avoided the after-school rush by getting rides from her friends since late freshman year, she couldn't help but feel the familiar panic of pushing through the crowds to board her bus in time. At this moment, she was desperate for time to slow down again.

Jess hadn't said a word about Xander yet. Violet quickly said her goodbyes to Emmy and Yvonne and quickly shuffled out of the room following Jess's lead. She figured going into the conversation and getting it over with quickly would be the better move compared to stalling by chit-chatting with her friends at the end of the day like usual. That was her strategy: Rip the band aid. Though to her surprise, her friend had not yet said a word.

As Jess exited the classroom, she made a left to head directly down the stairs and through the doors to the student parking lot. Violet followed for a few steps then said, "Wait."

"What?" Jess asked, pausing and looking over her shoulder at Violet.

"I need to get something from my locker."

Jess nodded and they both turned back, heading right down the hallway to the direction of Violet's locker.

She really hated where her locker was in relation to her classes. It was rather out of the way of the majority of her path. She spent most of her day just carrying around all of her books and folders to make it easy. She even got some extra big binders and added dividers for three classes in each so she only had to make one major swap during the day, usually after lunch. It took up a ton of space in her bag, regardless.

As they approached her locker, Jess still hadn't said a word. The freshmen were creating wind on either side of them as they walked deeper into the school while they hustled to get out.

Violet reached her locker and stared at the combination lock. She always turned it a few extra times before putting her combination in, just to make extra certain it had reset. Twenty four, spin back, counter-clockwise this time. Jess stood to her right, watching intently as she entered her combination. Pass zero, and stop at forty-five. Violet's palms felt clammy—Jess had to be upset with her, right? One more mini-twist back clockwise to land on nine.

She pulled up on the latch and swung the locker door open. She looked at Jess quickly. She appeared relaxed, but her eyes betrayed something else. Boredom? Perhaps irritation? Whatever it was, it was oddly reminiscent of the looks of those waiting in line at the post office or for a walk-up ATM. Dull and listless. It was jarring for Violet, but she maintained her composure, removing the books from her bag she knew she wouldn't need and replacing them with some packets and papers left on the top shelf. She wanted Jess to bring it up first.

She took one last look at her open locker door before deciding it was time to close it. The time that passed as she waited for Jess to finally acknowledge her recent and unexpected deflowering felt labored and exhausting, though based on the number of students in the hall at that moment, Violet determined the busses were probably only just closing their doors to leave the parking lot. This also meant the pile-up of student traffic would be beginning its own slow, stop-and-start parade onto the street. The girls would likely spend at least fifteen minutes baking in their car before starting the first leg of their journey home.

This knot in Violet's stomach twisted, swinging back and forth, banging against her other organs with every step they took.

Jess remained quiet as they went through the door. Without hesitation, she went straight to her car, parked in the third row over in the back half.

Cars were lined down every row, slowly filtering into the single-file line stopped at the light before they could turn onto the road, the lot was still completely packed with students who still hadn't had the good fortune to be let into the line. Had it really only been a few minutes?

Violet heard the locks pop at Jess's passenger door and opened it, setting her bag down first so it would rest between her legs as they drove. Jess nonchalantly entered her car and sat down. She inserted her key into the ignition, twisted it, and the engine came to life. She looked over her shoulder to see if there was any opening to back into. Of course, there wasn't.

She stayed looking out her back windshield, not speaking, focused on starting their drive home and not getting hit by another student.

Buzz buzz.

Violet didn't jump at the vibration but welcomed it. Finally, a little distraction from the tension between them.

She whipped her phone out of her back pocket and autonomously unlocked the screen, flipping to her messages. Open and highlighted, she read:

XANDER
Staying late today?

She looked at it, actually considering getting out of Jess's car to go fool around by the baseball fields somewhere with no explanation whatsoever. She really needed to stop daydreaming of dragging and dropping herself anywhere else, like rescuing a computer file from the trash bin, but all day that was her emotional craving.

"Texting Xander?" Jess finally broke her silence.

Violet looked over and noticed Jess had noticed her scrolling through her phone.

This was it, the big confrontation.

"Yeah, actually." She answered confidently.

Jess nodded and looked back over her shoulder to check for an opening.

"Is he inviting you over again?"

Violet considered her words carefully.

"Not exactly," she said, "We were just talking about hanging out after school sometime this week."

"Are you," there was a pause as Jess now considered her words carefully, "dating again?" That seemed right. It was non-threatening, and it got to the point.

Violet unintentionally scoffed and spoke, "No," while typing out her response to Xander. She felt like she'd answered that question one-hundred times in the last few hours alone, though she immediately regretted the tone she took as she said it.

VIOLET

Let's wait till I get my car this

weekend. :)

"Oh, I'm sorry," Jess started. "Forgive me for being confused, I've just heard some strange rumors going around today." The words were sincere but held a twinge of sarcasm. She did not make eye contact with Violet.

Suddenly, ripping the band aid felt more like poking the bear. She managed to make matters worse and she'd only said three things to Jess so far.

"Anyway, how's the GSA thing going?" Maybe a subject change was just the thing they needed to cut through the tension.

Jess glanced at her friend, issuing a look that said, "I know what you're doing," before finally noticing an opening as a beige pickup truck let her back into the line of hand-me-own cars thumping with music the students unwound.

The cacophony of songs overlapping each other was audible through the closed windows of

113

Jess's sedan. After the few words they'd just exchanged, it really didn't sound so bad.

As she shifted into drive and started following the path to the stoplight, Jess spoke, "I have a meeting with Principal Mick later this week to try and fast track everything. That's actually why I ended up in your classroom at the end of the day."

"What do you mean?"

"Over the weekend I was looking at the club roster, and I put together a list of all the teachers who weren't currently advising any clubs, so I reached out to some of them that I knew and asked if anyone was interested in advising for the GSA. Ms. Elliot responded right away and said she'd love to help out any way she could."

"So, what did you give her?"

"Some basic introductory information about starting a GSA that I found on their network website and a list of activities for some of our first meetings."

"Wow, you're really prepared," Violet said. She knew Jess was very motivated, but everything seemed to be moving at a faster-than-typical rate for her.

"Yeah, well, I need everything to be pre-planned and established before this meeting, and I really wanted some staff on my side."

The traffic moved a little quicker now as more cars filtered from the lot. They merged into the main lane and prepared to clear that first stoplight.

"On your side?" Violet's eyebrows raised.

"Yeah, well, I guess that nasty secretary thinks the school won't institute the club. She almost didn't take my form, so I asked to schedule a meeting with the principal. I don't want to risk her 'losing my form' or telling me she'll 'get to it later' and never doing it because she's a homophobic bigot."

Violet was surprised to hear this. How can someone work for a school and actively try to suppress a group of kids trying to support each other through some of the roughest times of their lives? Violet had experienced firsthand this day how blatantly teenagers can lie and spread secrets; she couldn't even imagine being in a position of a student being outed by mean kids with nothing better to do than snoop in other people's business.

"Do you think Mick will have a problem with it?" she asked.

"I don't know, but I'm going in prepared. I have my advisor, I have club activities planned, and it is a national organization. This way if he tries to fight it, I have ammo," she said, "Just in case." Violet was certain she added the words more to convince herself than anything. She seemed anxious about it, for sure.

They pulled through the green light and finally they were cruising down the road to head home.

"Do you have any potential members lined up? Maybe that could help," Violet offered.

Jess nodded. "Absolutely. A handful of kids from the student council want to offer support. My friend Dana, the one who does the plays, said a bunch of kids from the theatre department are interested, and I know a handful of students in band who I have been talking to about it. And you," she paused, "Right?"

"Of course, you can count on me." She felt the irony of the words. She had to imagine Jess felt pretty lied-to after hearing what had happened over the weekend.

"Good," Jess moved along. "Could you maybe make an announcement in choir too?"

"Yeah, definitely, and I actually think Yvonne is going to be on the newspaper team again. Maybe she can write an article or something to promote it?"

"Really? That'd be awesome. Can you send me her number?"

"On it," Violet gave the affirmative while scrolling through her phone to copy the contact into a message to Jess.

A few moments of silence passed again as Violet worked through her phone. The mood had certainly lightened. Perhaps that's what gave Jess the courage to finally ask.

The car had stopped as they waited at a red light, and Violet noticed some gray clouds in the sky ahead.

"So, do you want to tell me what happened this weekend, or what?"

CHAPTER ELEVEN

The engine rumbled beneath their feet as Violet began developing her response in her head.

"It's really not as serious as everyone is making it out to be. There was no sneaking out of the house or rendezvous in his parent's bed. Just two friends losing their virginity—it was just a thing that happened." As Violet spoke, she began to experience the freedom of speaking in a closed-in vehicle. No one was there to overhear her; she didn't have to choose her words so carefully. It was just Jess.

"And I know I made a big deal about how it wasn't going to happen, and I'm really sorry about that; it's just that the more I thought about it, I really thought it would be a good thing for me to get this whole big thing done and over with someone I really trust. Xander is a good friend, and now I don't have to worry about regretting it!" This was the first time she tried to honestly explain her thought process to someone. Surely Jess would understand why she made her decision and how her thoughts on the matter changed.

Or maybe she was dead wrong.

"You don't regret it?" Her voice was stern and rigid like she'd cast a line into Violet's mouth to forcefully reel the truth out of her, but she didn't budge.

"Vi, we've known each other too long for you to think I can't tell when you're kidding yourself," Jess said quietly, keeping her eyes locked on the road ahead.

"Well, I'm sorry I don't want to lose my virginity to someone who will dump me the next day," Violet mumbled to herself but just loud enough for Jess to hear and punctuating it with a cross of her arms.

"So you decided to lose your virginity to someone who *already* dumped you?"

Those words stung a little more than Violet expected, particularly because it felt sort of true. The reason she and Xander had broken up was because he'd seemed a bit distant. She thought he was going to break up with her, so she just asked him.

All he did was shrug at her. He wasn't sure, and when Violet pressed him, he only said he wasn't sure he was "doing the boyfriend thing right." Then they didn't speak for a few days.

It had felt weird for Violet and Xander to not speak, even for a few days. They were a sweet sort of "friends-first" couple that always depended on each other for advice in freshman year. After those first few days, Violet got bored of trying to avoid him and just sent him a simple text.

VIOLET
Friends?

Xander agreed and that was the story of her first break-up. They had only dated a few months, they never said "the L-word", and they just picked up their friendship where they left off. She always wondered though, what would have happened if Xander hadn't suddenly started second-guessing his ability to be a good boyfriend? Would they still be together? Would they have had an even nastier break-up and not stayed friends? In that way, it did feel like he initiated the end of their relationship, even if everything turned out okay.

The stinging didn't last long before it started to boil under her skin. Jess was supposed to be her confidant. It was easier to be honest with her when she didn't immediately interact with Violet's classmates. She felt as though she'd been kicked in the gut, so she impulsively decided to kick her back.

"Look, Jess, I said I'm sorry. Maybe if you had a *real* boyfriend, you'd be a bit more understanding."

That shut her up really quickly.

Though Jess seemed so perfect on paper, she had her flaws. She had transferred into the high school from the local Catholic school when she was a freshman and Violet was still in middle school as an 8th grader.

When Jess got to high school, she didn't know anyone, and she very quickly latched on to the first group of kids who accepted her. She felt the need to impress them and be interesting, thinking her life as a private schoolgirl wasn't the type of thing that interested public school kids, so she had a tendency to embellish the truth a bit.

The most notable lie was her rich boyfriend. She used to tell her friends crazy stories about how they'd go sailing in his dad's boat at the lake, how they saw each other all the time because their dads worked together, even though he went to another school, and she even had a few pictures of him she'd show off.

When her new friends wanted to meet him, she went straight to Violet to confess.

"I don't have a boyfriend," she'd said so breathlessly.

"He dumped you?" Violet asked.

"No. I never had one. I wanted to seem cool or something. I don't know, it was stupid, but now my friends want to meet him and I don't know what to do."

Violet had consoled Jess and told her she'd keep the secret. She said she'd vouch for her and say she'd met him before if her friends ever asked and told her to just say they broke up.

That seemed to work. Jess got to keep her interesting story of her rich ex-boyfriend and her new friends, but the topic always sent her into fits of extreme embarrassment. Violet had always settled her by saying that everyone does silly things and tells wild lies when they're young. It must have hurt Jess to suddenly judge her for this.

"Fine," Jess mumbled, eyes glued ahead, "As long as you're okay with all those rumors going around."

"They'll die down in a week," Violet replied, still heated, deep down, however, a part of her already writhed with guilt for what she had said. It was a low blow, and she knew it. Yet, in the heat of the moment, she didn't really care.

Jess pulled into the Gray's driveway and parked her car.

Violet quickly exited the vehicle but stopped before closing the door to say one more thing, "I sent you Yvonne's contact."

Jess nodded with a dull face. "Thanks."

Violet closed the door and headed inside.

Her dad worked late on Mondays; she knew she'd have to make her own dinner. She slid between the stacks of items lining the floors of their chaotic garage, narrowly missing an aggressive stubbing of her toe on some boxes that may have contained holiday decorations. She never really knew.

She threw her backpack on the kitchen floor and grabbed a snack from the cabinet to give her mouth something to do other than scream.

She chewed angrily as she stomped up the stairs and sat at her desk, opening the screen of her laptop to navigate through her social media, hopefully finding some videos of cute animals to ease her nerves; that always seemed to help.

As her screen loaded, she noticed she still had a tab open from last night. It was the listing for the car she'd planned to get that weekend. She tabbed the arrows to look through the pictures again.

The seats in the back definitely laid flat so things could be stored in the trunk (or to create a spot for two people to lie down.)

Her head cocked to one side, wondering if everyone else got out of their car, laid down the seats, and then got busy. That seemed somewhat like a mood-killer.

She tried to imagine what it might be like to lean the front seat all the way back instead. Perhaps that would make an easier get-away if they were going to get caught. The thought of a cop pulling up and tapping on a fogged-up window while she had every one of her nooks and crannies out on display gave her a little shudder.

Maybe she'd need to wear a skirt or something.

She moused up to the address bar, but before she started typing, she was hit with a better idea. She clicked on the menu button, opening a collection of new buttons including the one she was hoping for: new incognito window.

The black-lined box reflected off her eyes as she went up to the address bar and typed in the only website she imagined would be able to help her: Pornhub. Frankly, it was the only porn website she really knew.

Immediately she was flooded with images of other women's nooks and crannies. She winced a bit but found the search bar and typing in "Car Sex".

She imagined she would find enough results to help her get some better ideas of what to expect; the majority seemed to have the woman straddling the man in the front seat. Though there were some others with girls laid down on their backs like they were in the back of a hatchback.

On a whim, she clicked one and muted her computer.

It was a matter of seconds before penetration had begun and within exactly twelve seconds of the video starting, she exited the incognito window.

Of course the video didn't show how the couple set up; that's not what people came to that website for. She felt stupid even imagining she'd get some sort of director's cut with behind-the-scenes footage of some amateur pornographic film.

She recalled a rumor of this sophomore at the high school who apparently watched porn in the bathroom during lunch. She couldn't imagine ever doing something like that. She'd barely made it through fifteen seconds of one video, let alone watching several in a day with other people around. It seemed strange to her that it wouldn't get boring.

She shook the thoughts from her head and went to plug in her phone. It was at about thirty percent, but figured she'd plug it in while she could and get some homework done while she listened to music.

She tapped the app for her favorite streaming service which was set up to start playing from the Top

Hits from the 80's to Now Station immediately. She stood up to head downstairs and retrieve her backpack with her history homework packet inside when she noticed the song playing.

Like a Virgin, by Madonna.

What a coincidence.

She sighed and sat back down at her desk. There was no way she would be able to get this out of her head. She'd heard her dad say something once about listening to a song you had stuck in your head to be able to get it out.

She navigated back to a website so recently frequented it should have been bookmarked by now: *Cosmopolitan.*

She knew exactly what article to look up, and following the advice delineated, she sent the following text:

VIOLET

Tell me what you want to do to me ;)

And she waited for Xander's reply.

CHAPTER TWELVE

By Friday, the collection of messages between Violet and Xander had amassed into a cesspool of hormones and innuendos, though upon a quick scroll, one might have noticed some missing messages.

XANDER
I want to see you

VIOLET
Wearing what? ;)

XANDER
Nothing please

VIOLET
Only since you asked so nice. What do you want me to do?

XANDER
Surprise me :)

Id give anything to have you on my
bed like that right now

Over the course of the week, the two had laid some rather explicit ground rules for the benefit of their friendship. The number one rule from Violet, in no uncertain terms, was that any and all photos needed to be deleted immediately upon receipt.

As their planned rendezvous approached, throughout the day, she found herself significantly less nervous than the first time. This time she'd be ready.

She sat in the passenger seat of her father's car as he drove them to the sales lot. The ride had been mostly quiet with the radio playing rock music, making the mood a bit more casual, even with his random anecdotes about car crashes and dumb choices his classmates made back when he was in high school.

"You know, my buddy Kent always used to drive a group of kids home after school. They were always really rowdy, and one day one of them punched him in the arm and he got distracted trying to hit him back. Ran straight into a tree."

Violet assumed this was supposed to convey a message to her about being careful with the people she drove around, but the image of a passenger punching the driver led her thoughts to Jess. She did deliver a pretty big metaphorical punch during their last drive. They hadn't spoken all week. Jess had her after-school activities during the middle of the week, and Violet was getting her car, so they hadn't had a ride home together since Monday. It suddenly hit Violet that with her own car she wouldn't be needing anyone to drive her home anymore; she could take herself.

This made her a bit sad; perhaps she'd need to find some way to apologize.

"And Violet," Mr. Gray commanded her attention, pulling her out of her daydreams, "No boyfriends in this car, got it?"

Violet smiled. "No worries, dad. I don't have any boyfriends to speak of." It wasn't technically a lie, Xander was just her friend.

Mr. Gray parked near the little rundown building where a salesman waited outside for him, waving. Violet exited the car with her father and followed him out as the two men started discussing paperwork.

Violet looked around and spotted her little hatchback parked at the side of the building, ready for her to test drive. She wandered over to it, smiling wide.

This was what she wanted from her junior year: a car, a real job, and freedom. Sex was really low on the radar of wants only a week ago. So much had changed so quickly.

Her mind was a non-stop looping of messages she and Xander had exchanged throughout the week.

XANDER
Do you want to do anything different
this time?

VIOLET
I have some things in mind…

XANDER
Like?

VIOLET
Idk, like foreplay or something?

XANDER
Oh yeah. I can make that happen :) I
know the best place to park too

One thing Violet knew, she wasn't good at expressing exactly what she wanted. Honestly, she still wasn't sure. Every article she'd read in *Cosmo* seemed to imply that she needed to have a little solo playtime for her to figure that out, but she really never felt like doing that. She'd made a point of telling herself that at some point, she'd have to, no matter how much of a chore it felt like.

Thankfully, Xander was open to feedback and agreed this time would be undoubtedly better. This only further solidified that Xander was the right person to do this with, even if she didn't have any real sexual desire for him.

As she test drove her new car with her dad's friend in the passenger seat and her dad in the back, she tried not to think about the encounter that was to occur shortly after they left the lot in the very spot her father sat. She was afraid that somehow he would realize her plans and try to keep her at home.

Thankfully, however, that didn't seem to be the case. Her father just repeated over and over the privilege and the responsibility of having her own car, dangling the keys in front of her face as the salesman finalized the paperwork.

Violet nodded nonstop, following the movement of the keys back and forth like she intended to be hypnotized, and it truly felt that way as Mr. Gray placed the keys into her hand, opening the door to the new chapter of her life.

As she opened the literal door to her new car, she turned to her dad. "You mind if I take it out for a ride before heading home?"

Her father inhaled deeply before conceding. "Fine, but be home before dark."

"Deal!" And with that, an excited Violet shimmied into her driver's seat. She typed a quick text message to her FWB.

VIOLET
On my way. Be ready ;)

She smiled at herself in the rearview mirror, noting her glowing demeanor before backing out onto the road and heading off.

Xander was waiting for her outside, sitting on the step to his front door. He smiled and waved, approaching her car and slipping in through the passenger side door.

"Hey," she smiled cheerfully, "What do you think?"

"It's awesome," he commented, "you ready for this?"

With a nod, Violet had taken off to the center of town where the baseball fields sat. There were four of them with multiple entrances, one of which led to a parking lot completely invisible from the road (courtesy of the surrounding trees) and usually completely empty outside of the Saturday morning tee-ball games. This was the go-to parking spot in town which was immediately made evident by the two visible condoms casually tossed onto the cement in the parking lot. Violet didn't even want to imagine how many she'd find closer to the trees.

With the car parked, she dropped her arms and looked at Xander, waiting for him to make the first move. In spite of how confident she had been moments earlier, suddenly things were awkward again.

"So, I got something for you," Xander said to break the silence.

Violet cocked her head to one side and creased her forehead. "What do you mean?"

Xander reached into his pocket, removing a long white piece of plastic with a bulbous end wrapped in bright neon orange duct tape.

"What is that?" She genuinely could not understand.

Xander, instead of responding verbally, flipped a switch upward on the right of the gift, causing it to begin vibrating. He was smiling a little too confidently.

It was an electric toothbrush with the bristles wrapped in duct tape.

She immediately burst into laughter. "Dude, I'm not using that!"

"Well, I was thinking I could use it on you, for foreplay or whatever," he explained.

Violet shook her head, "Absolutely not." She took the MacGyvered vibrator from him and stuffed it in her bag, tucked neatly behind her driver's seat before kicking one leg over the gearshift and straddling him. She leaned over and whispered in his ear, "We don't need it."

He shuddered a little as she blew a soft stream of air into his ear. From all the articles she'd read from the male perspective, this was apparently super erotic. This had proven true.

She kissed his neck and fumbled with the zipper on his jeans. So far, car sex was a lot more cramped than the videos on Pornhub lead her to believe.

Within a second, she had flopped forward, knocking her head into Xander's jaw. He had pulled the lever to lean the seat backward with no warning, causing a miniature collision of their heads.

Violet sat up with her hand on her head, only to whack the back of her head on the roof of the car. This was the definition of a horrible start.

"Ooh, I'm so sorry!" Xander exclaimed, sitting himself up on his elbows and rubbing his jaw with his own hand.

"It's fine," Violet ignored it, pushing through the pounding she felt and returning her full attention to his zipper, managing to get it undone with the use of both her eyes.

Xander slid both of his hands up her skirt, slipping his thumbs underneath the waistband of her thong and dragged them down her legs slowly while she unpacked his boxers.

He immediately relaxed, leaning backward to enjoy Violet's handwork.

She attempted to gracefully pull her underwear off herself completely with one hand occupied. Once the task was completed, Xander reached forward with his right hand, pushing his fingers into her with her legs spread wide on top of his.

Unsure of the reason, she immediately reached for his wrist and moved his hands away, leaning over top of him further to start kissing his neck again.

With a hint of confusion in his face, he reached into his pocket for a condom, rolling it over himself so he'd be prepared for what would come next.

Violet lifted her hips and angled herself over Xander, sitting herself on top of him so he'd slide into her with minimal resistance.

She let out a whisper of a moan and looked up to Xander's eyes, half rolled into the back of his head. She raised and lowered her hips again, getting a little louder. *Cosmo* said men liked it when women were loud.

She was analyzing his reaction when he grabbed her hips, bracing himself to thrust powerfully into her repeatedly before letting out his own scream of ecstasy while Violet followed his lead.

He laid limp under her as she rolled off, retrieving her panties from the floor of the car, deciding to slip them into her bag, rather than replace them as she wondered about how clean these carpets really were.

She straightened her skirt out and smoothed her hair while Xander opened the door to dispose of their contraceptive.

Violet frowned. Sure, it was a disgusting thing to keep in the car, but she didn't want to be part of the crowd that just threw their juices out into the wilderness. She stayed quiet in spite of this.

Xander turned to her, smiling as he packed himself back into his pants, zipping everything back in. "That was way better than last time," he confessed. He had a look in his eye like Violet had when she looked at herself for the first time as a car owner. "Right?"

Violet smiled widely. "Yes, absolutely." There was a hint of truth to that statement. Though the start was rough, it was a much better experience than the last time. But why didn't she want him to touch her? Why did she take his hand away? At the moment, it felt instinctual, but now she wasn't sure.

She did everything right: she was flirty, she was loud, they engaged in a little foreplay. It lasted longer; there was a little more movement, yet still, something felt off.

"So it was good for you?" Xander asked, looking rather proud of himself.

Violet nodded slowly. "Yeah," she said with a hint of uncertainty, but Xander didn't notice. He sat happily on cloud nine while Violet anxiously wondered why, if she'd done everything right, she felt so apathetic.

CHAPTER THIRTEEN

Over the course of the next few weeks, Violet had become somewhat obsessive over her sexual appetite, or lack thereof. The whispers of her name in the hall had died down, passing over like all other instances of a busted cherry. She and Xander had a relatively well-established routine by now, which most of her peers simply referred to as a "booty call", but while Xander seemed motivated to meet for his own sexual satisfaction, it had turned into a bit of an experiment for Violet.

She dwelled incessantly on how uncomfortable she was with Xander touching her below the belt. It was like a flood of anxiety overcame her every time he tried to give her any special attention. She usually played it off as if the moment was more about him and his pleasure, but she knew she couldn't continue to fight his hands away.

That had to be the reason she wasn't enjoying sex.

As she set her knees on either side of his hips, toying lightly with the collar of his shirt, she spoke softly to him, each word dripping with drawls and lingering with a deep sense of sensuality. "Do you think this time you could give me a little special attention?"

Like a dog who had been offered a treat, Xander nodded aggressively, licking his lips in preparation to delicately trace the lines between her legs with his tongue. He swung her legs over his shoulders, laying her on her back, and resting his head against her inner thighs as if they were earmuffs.

He slowly dragged the tip of his tongue around her while she laid, staring at the ceiling of her car, padding in gray felt, waiting for the crashing waves of pleasure to hit her like a ton of bricks. As usual, they never came.

The very next encounter following that had gone no better.

Xander reached into his jacket pocket, retrieving a small package of Listerine breath strips and placing one on his tongue.

"What are you doing?" Violet asked with a knitted brow.

"I just thought it would make it taste better." Xander looked matter-of-factly at her, seeming to miss the obvious demonstration of offense on her face.

"What do you mean? What does it taste like?!" she exclaimed, her voice cracking a bit in a high-pitched tone.

"Oh, uh," he paused, "I guess it tastes like… batteries."

Were it not for her desperation to feel a sense of satisfaction from their rendezvous, she would have left right then. Of course, she was willing to try anything to finally experience sex the right way. Once again, she moaned and groaned her way to the end of the endeavor, feeling a tad more numb than usual, which she attributed to the burning mint flavoring on her clitoris.

After all her misadventures, she couldn't help but sigh in relief as she stopped in the bathroom before lunch the following Monday. She never thought she'd be so excited to have her period.

VIOLET

No meetup tomorrow, on my .

XANDER

Message received lol

Finally, she felt relaxed. She could worry about what was wrong with her another day. The cramps were surprisingly welcome as she leaned over the lunch table, eating soggy cafeteria pizza with cheese that never seemed to actually melt. Yvonne was telling her about how excited she was to share the article she wrote for the school newspaper.

"The new website automatically sends a weekly newsletter to all the students with links to the newest articles. Mine should be in there tonight. I think it turned out really great." She seemed genuinely excited.

Jess had reached out to her to publish the article on the GSA, and while Violet hadn't spent too much time with Jess in the last few weeks, she did send her a quick apology to clear the air. Of course, it was accepted, with an apology in return for being judgmental, and they moved on. Jess wasn't the type to hold a grudge.

"Cool, I'll look out for it." Violet smiled. The conversation halted as they each bit off another piece of their lunches.

"I do actually have something else I want to talk to you about," Yvonne spoke, covering her mouth as she chewed the last few bites of her peanut butter and jelly sandwich.

"Yeah?"

She nodded. "I was talking to Steven last night and he said he has a friend who'd be willing to drive him into town so we could have a real date that isn't on a forest path about twelve steps away from deer pee."

Violet snorted slightly as Yvonne continued.

"His name is Derek, and he's really tall and funny. He plays lacrosse, actually."

Violet nodded along, starting to understand exactly where Yvonne was going, as she snapped into a pretzel stick off her lunch tray.

"So we were thinking we could maybe do a double date? Me and Steven and you and Derek?"

Violet continued nodding, swishing the dry pretzel around in her mouth, wanting to swallow before responding.

"I know you're still kind of hooking up with Xander or whatever, so I wasn't sure. I just wanted to ask." She seemed so nervous. Violet knew she was afraid she'd say "no" and she wouldn't be able to see Steven during the week.

Xander was not her boyfriend and their relationship as fuckbuddies shouldn't really dictate whether she starts dating someone else, but they'd never really discussed this. When did their arrangement need to end? When did the benefits cease in relation to beginning a serious relationship with someone else?

"I mean, he's not my boyfriend, I can do whatever I want, but I don't know. We never talked about this happening. Maybe I should text him?" she questioned aloud.

Yvonne nodded. "Take your time. We were thinking about Thursday, but just let me know."

Violet's phone sat between her fingers within seconds and she tapped her message to Xander, punctuating it without a question mark on purpose.

VIOLET

Hey. Y asked if I wanted to go on a
double date with her.

XANDER

Cool. With?

VIOLET

She's seeing this guy she met
camping and he's got a single
friend.

XANDER

Ah. Well have fun then. Let me know
if it goes anywhere lol

As much as she didn't love the sex, she did love Xander for how direct he was, even if it meant spending a few hours at night wondering if it was normal for your vagina to taste like batteries.

XANDER

btw, Trav is having a party this
weekend. You wanna come?

VIOLET

Definitely, sounds fun.

XANDER

I think Lindsey is planning it, so
prepare for games. Bring whoever.

There wasn't a doubt in her mind. As quickly as their fling had begun, it would just as quickly end with no hard feelings.

"What's he saying?" Yvonne asked, packing the remnants of her lunch back into her bag before the bell rang.

"No worries. I can go on the date, for sure." Violet smiled.

"Really? Yay!" She leaned over and gave Violet a big bear hug and she overflowed with excitement. "Does Thursday work for you?"

"You bet. Just text me what time and where and I'll be there."

With those words, Yvonne wasted no time whipping out her phone to send affirmative texts to Steven and solidifying their plans.

"He also said Lindsey and Travis are throwing a party this weekend. You should come if you aren't going camping again."

Yvonne frowned a bit. "I'm not sure yet, I'll have to ask my parents. I'm sure Emmy would love to go though," she noted, chuckling as added in her last thought.

"Oh yeah, I totally forgot her punishment is up this weekend. I wonder if her mom would even let her go?"

"We both know she's not going to tell her mom the truth about where she is going."

The girls laughed as the bell chimed, signaling the group of students to half-heartedly stand up and traverse the halls back to a desk for the second half of the day.

Yvonne waved her goodbyes and the two girls headed down separate hallways and into their respective classrooms.

As Violet walked, she started really thinking about the implications of going on a date with this guy, especially a stranger she'd never seen or met before. A weeknight date surely wouldn't result in a one-night-stand, no matter how many write-ins *Cosmo* posted about it, but was it possible the date could lead somewhere? Could she possibly fall in love with this guy?

She wondered if that is what was missing. Perhaps the reason she never really enjoyed sex with Xander was that she didn't have any strong, romantic love for him. It would make sense given the term "making love". It's possible she wasn't broken at all, but that the best sex is meaningful sex.

She made a note to herself to do a little more research that night. Had it not been for the cramping in her lower stomach, she's certain she would have had a little bounce in her step at that revelation; she wasn't wrong, she just wasn't in love.

CHAPTER FOURTEEN

Once Thursday had rolled around, Violet was feeling more positive. She had made arrangements to leave after school with Yvonne to head to their favorite local ice cream place, The Shake Shoppe. There, the boys would meet them around three.

Steven and Derek lived about thirty miles from the girls, down in a rural town a bit closer to the campground where Yvonne's family had their trailer parked. Their school let out around two, giving them plenty of time to drive while Violet and Yvonne only had to take a short walk down the road to the Shake Shoppe.

Violet left her car parked in the school lot as they walked. Yvonne tapped on her phone, texting back and forth for updates from Steven while Violet was left to overthink. This was the first date she had been on in quite a while, and it felt especially strange to no longer depend on her father to pick her up.

She reached out her arm to press the pedestrian crossing button on the stoplight. Yvonne looked so at peace, waiting for another message to come while Violet impatiently tapped her foot, waiting for the bright red hand to disappear. The Shake Shoppe sat basking in the sunlight right ahead of them, looking so tempting she might have jay-walked had it not been for the after-school traffic.

She struggled to imagine what she'd talk about with this boy. She'd only seen a few photos of Derek on social media. He was handsome, obviously athletic. He had dark hair with a short hairstyle, much like the boys from MROTC had. He had really piercing blue eyes, almost intimidating, and even in a social media picture, he seemed to be judging her. He also rarely smiled in his photos. This left Violet with a sour taste in her mouth. She genuinely believed a smile was the most attractive thing a man could wear.

"He said they'll be here in fifteen minutes!" Yvonne's smile widened with every passing moment. Violet didn't respond; she had a gut feeling the majority of the double date would be spent finding something in common with Derek while Steven and Yvonne made googly eyes at each other while trading spoonfuls of their ice cream back and forth. She knew better than to be bitter, though. Yvonne had finally found someone that made her happy who she felt confident around.

As much as she hated to admit it to herself, she was feeling a tad jealous.

She pulled out her phone for a distraction. Luckily, one had just come.

XANDER
Good luck on your date :)

Violet gave a small smile and shook her head slightly. Xander had been teasing her all week and made a few comments about how he needed to find a girlfriend now that she was off finding a boyfriend. The majority of his jokes seemed to be based around the idea that since this was a blind date, he might be a serial killer, and Steven had been his accomplice the whole time. She wondered if he was trying to get her to back out or not.

She typed a reply.

> VIOLET
>
> I'll send you an SOS if he tries to abduct me or anything ;P

XANDER

Well he definitely will if you get into his car!!

> VIOLET
>
> Then we'll just have to use my car if we go anywhere!

Violet thought that was a clever response at first.

XANDER

In your car, eh? So it's that kind of date ;)

She knew he was joking. She knew he was trying to be funny. But, as she read those words, she couldn't help her mind starting to wander.

This wasn't some Tinder hook-up, this was a blind date between teenagers. On a *school night*. It wasn't like she'd be heading back to his place with him, and he definitely wouldn't be heading back to hers. Somehow, though, all she could think of was Jess reminding her of how teenage boys think. Was sex on the table at all?

No. She thought. *It can't be.* There were just too many obstacles—too many risks.

When Violet glanced up to the crosswalk, she noticed the red light at the other end of the crosswalk blinking. She and Yvonne had been so caught up in their conversations that they'd missed the signal change.

"Yv, come on," she called as she shuffled her way into the street with their remaining ten seconds. Yvonne noticed and quickly sauntered after, still smiling at the words on her pocket-sized screen.

Violet guided an entranced Yvonne onto one of the outdoor benches where they would wait for their dates to arrive, and where Violet knew she'd have another ten minutes (at least) alone with her thoughts.

She glanced back at the last message from Xander. She wouldn't have sex with him, not even if the opportunity presented itself. She didn't want to. At this point, she wasn't even certain she was attracted to him in any way. She went on this date as a favor to Yvonne, it wasn't about her and Derek. She was like the spare tire you kept in the trunk of your car to keep things rolling in case of emergencies.

Still, she couldn't help but wonder if he'd try anything, or even if he'd ask if she was a virgin or not. And what would she say? Would telling the truth give him a different impression of her? Would he expect something sordid?

What if she lied? What if she said she was a virgin? What would he think of her then? That she's a prude? Or maybe that no one ever *wanted* to have sex with her?

Her distraction clearly did not help to ease her nerves. She quickly typed a response.

VIOLET
Wouldn't you like to know?

She put her phone on silent, sliding it into her school bag where she wouldn't be so tempted to grab it and folded her hands in her lap, looking down the street expectantly as if she was looking for them.

"What kind of car does he drive?" Violet asked.

Yvonne shrugged. If Violet didn't know better, she'd assume Yvonne was actually in love with her phone the way she was holding it, almost like she was doting on a small animal.

After a few minutes of Violet staring down the street, Yvonne joined her, jumping up from the bench and waving her arm widely over her head to attract the attention of a passing orange pickup truck which rolled slightly too far past the entrance to the Shake Shoppe.

The girls watched as Derek bobbed the car awkwardly back and forth performing what could only be accurately described as a thirteen-point turn in the tiny parking lot of the neighboring dentist's office. Finally, he turned around completely and came back out to turn into one of the correct parking spaces.

Violet decided she wouldn't tell him the parking lot went around the back and out on the other side.

The boys got out of the car and Yvonne excitedly greeted Steven with a hug. They looked adorable together. They complimented each other rather well. Yvonne's long and slender body with her short dark hair perfectly windswept against Steven's sandy blonde locks and sharp jaw made them look like a movie-star couple. They looked like the kind of couple who camped together with naturally sun-bronzed skin and toned arms from several canoe trips.

Then Derek left the car. He actually smiled when he saw her, contrasting his pictures right away. He was a little shorter than Steven, but absolutely more built.

Yvonne turned her back to Steven for only a moment to perform introductions. "Violet, this is Steven," she said, motioning to him.

Steven put a hand out to shake. Violet shook his hand one time up and down. "I've heard a lot about you!" There was a pause, "All good things."

He had a very natural smile. "Thank God!" He laughed a little. "And this is my friend, Derek."

Derek waved. Violet waved back. "Violet." She gave her name as she realized she hadn't yet. He seemed nice enough. "Nice to meet you." She offered her most genuine smile. Actually meeting him was far less intimidating than it had been in her head.

"And you." He returned the sentiment as the foursome made their way to the line inside the store. Yvonne and Steven walked in step at the head of the group, with Derek just behind and Violet falling behind him, slightly off on a diagonal so they weren't quite shoulder-to-shoulder as the couple ahead of them were. The small talk had begun.

"So what's good here?" Steven started.

"Everything! They have these things called Blasters; you can mix up to three toppings in any flavor of ice cream they have!" Yvonne reported excitedly.

"Is that what you get?" Derek asked.

"Always! Chocolate ice cream, Reese's cups, Reese's pieces, and sometimes pretzels."

"Sweet and salty's always been her favorite," Violet added, not exactly to Derek, but more so to Steven.

This gave the conversation a strange atmosphere. It was almost as if Violet and Derek were individual third-wheels who hadn't yet realized they could all fit in the car at once.

Violet ordered a vanilla cone with sprinkles. That was the first time Derek said something directly to her. "Vanilla ice cream?" He seemed incredulous.

She self-consciously looked at her cone, holding it back a little to better assess it as a whole. "Yeah," she admitted. "Is that bad?"

Derek still had a strange look on his face. "I mean no, but out of all the flavors, you picked vanilla?"

"It's my favorite." Violet's tone was a mix of defensive and dejected. She kept her eyes on the cone.

He put his hands up near his shoulder, fingers wide like he was surrendering and shrugging at the same time. "Hey, I mean, there's nothing wrong with that. It just seems a little boring."

Her first impression had been formed; it wasn't stellar.

The conversation continued in a corner booth where the sets of friends took turns sharing stories with one another; starting with how they'd met.

Derek and Steven played off of one another, telling a story they'd obviously told a few times before about the two of them on their peewee flag football team. Derek had tried some professional-level tackles on him after having gone to his first NFL game with his dad the weekend before.

While he spoke, Violet watched him. He talked loudly, probably too loudly for how close they were, but he had a really great and really strong laugh that made her give up at least a little chuckle every time his voice echoed off the walls.

He had really straight teeth, but somewhat yellowed. She didn't want to judge; hers definitely weren't perfect, but she did notice. It was almost as obvious as Steven and Yvonne holding hands under the table. Violet couldn't help but wonder why they were trying to hide it.

As their date wrapped up, the girls followed the boys out to the hideous orange truck. Yvonne not so subtly followed Steven to the passenger side. Violet assumed they wanted a little privacy, and rocked back on her heels and bit with a forced smile as she was suddenly left alone with Derek.

"So, can I text you sometime?" he asked. Violet wondered why; it wasn't like they'd totally hit it off on their first meeting.

She politely nodded, fumbling to grab her phone from her bag as it weighed her down with school books. As she unlocked the device, she was met with a notification, actually, about twelve notifications. Xander hadn't responded, but Emmy had sent a series of interview questions, clearly growing restless with her punishment and lack of freedom.

EMMY
How's it goooooooing?

What's his last name again? I can't find him
on insta.
Why aren't you responding? :(
Does that mean it's going well?
Is he hot?
Hotter than Steven?
Found him. Sweet Jesus, he is RIPPED
Mentally undressing these pics as we speak.
;P
I'd kill for a man with that body.
He could break me in half and I'd say thank
you.
I'm drooling over the abs

She glanced up, blushing deep, making a
point to look at his stomach where his abs hid beneath
his shirt at least briefly. He was absolutely attractive,
objectively so, but even then she was definitely not
mentally undressing him in the ice cream shop.

Was he mentally undressing her?

Derek had one hand extended, hoping to grab
her phone so he could type in his number. She clicked
open a new message and set the phone in his palm
where he started typing.

Violet gave him one more all-over glance,
drinking in his every line, every detail, even noting

the way his shirt fell over his muscles, and yet, she never wondered what laid beneath those clothes.

She creased her brow slightly as she thought to herself how normal that was. Surely the majority of people didn't do that; that was just her crazy friend Emmy with the wild sex-drive.

Certainly, she was normal.

CHAPTER FIFTEEN

By Saturday, Violet and Derek had only exchanged a few texts.

DEREK
hey

VIOLET
Hey

DEREK
how was your day?

VIOLET
Good. Yours?

DEREK
cool. mine was good. doing anything fun this weeknd?

VIOLET
Just going to a party.

DEREK
cool cool.

Violet thought back on it as she combed through her warm curls, freshly formed by a curling iron. She considered inviting him, but something about the two of them together just didn't click. Definitely not as perfect a fit as Yvonne and Steven seemed to be. Looking back on their "first date" felt a little bit like a toddler interlocking two incorrect puzzle pieces; they touched in a few places, but there was some uncomfortable space left over.

Her phone buzzed.

EMMY

I'M DYING. COME FASTER.

Violet smiled and whipped the bathroom door open so she could gallop down the stairs and select the shoes she'd wear from the hall closet. She'd decided on a cropped purple shirt with black and gray stripes and some ripped jeans. Her eyes bounced back and forth between a pair of white Keds and silver sandals.

Sandals. She decided, wanting to look a bit flashier for the first major party of the year.

In her friend group, ragers weren't exactly common. Two or three of their friends would bring some wine coolers, unceremoniously lifted from their parent's freezer, and the rest was just debaucherous games and conversation.

Lindsey, their host for the evening, was the Games Mistress. She wanted things to run smoothly, skipping as much dead time as possible. If everything went correctly, there would be a clear routine that the evening followed, starting with Spin the Bottle, moving to Truth or Dare, and ending with Seven Minutes in Heaven.

Violet blew her dad a kiss, telling him she'd be back in the morning. As far as he knew, she was staying the night at Emmy's place, and when she said, "I'm heading to Emmy's!" it wasn't technically a lie.

Mr. Gray did not care much for Mrs. Morales and would go to great lengths to avoid talking with her on the phone, as such, he rarely checked with her when Violet said she'd be staying the night with Emmy, even if he suspected she was lying. She was a bit overbearing, even to another parent.

Emmy practically sprinted into the passenger seat once Violet had pulled into her driveway, waving innocently at her mother, standing with her arms crossed and a knitted brow outside of their front door.

"Bye, mom! See you tomorrow!" Emmy called out of her window, rolling it up, and mumbling to Violet as exasperated, "Dude, drive."

Violet nodded, and put her car in reverse, waving to Mrs. Morales as she backed away. With the windows rolled up, she wasn't sure, but it sure looked like she'd hollered, "Both hands on the wheel!" before heading back inside.

As they rounded the corner out of sight, Emmy began stripping out of her pants.

"What are you doing?" Violet asked, keeping her eyes ahead.

"What do you think? I'm changing! Mom wouldn't let me leave in my shorts." She shimmied a pair of booty shorts up her legs and unzipped her hoodie to reveal a low-cut black tank-top with a lacy, pink bralette peeking out of the top—classically Emmy.

As she swiped a sparkly gloss on her lips, Violet pulled into Travis's neighborhood, spotting the party from several houses away, made obvious by the chain of cars parked along the right side of the street.

She scanned the road for an open space, aiming for whichever had the shortest walk. As she pulled off to the side to park, Emmy tossed her purse filled with her more modest wardrobe into the back seat.

"Ready?" she asked.

"You bet." And the girls left the car, following the trail of vehicles to their destination.

The front door was unlocked with a sign taped to the screen.

Come in! Follow the music!

Once inside, it was a right turn down the hallway and into the first door on the left. This led to the basement, the hub of the party. The room was lightly dabbled in guests, some overlapping as they lounged on the basement furniture. Music played with a rather unimpressive bass so the guests could chat casually over it. Multi-colored lights danced around the room from a black plastic ball on a side table in the corner. It went mostly unnoticed, outshone by the overhead lights that were sill on.

Lindsey squealed upon recognition of her newest attendees. "Now we're only missing Yvonne and her new man!"

Emmy shook her head. "No, Yvonne's not coming. I think she and Steven wanted some *alone time*." She drew out those final words, sticking her tongue out and thrusting her hips forward a few times to ensure the message was clear.

Violet held back a roll of her eyes as she recalled Yvonne's text message to their group-chat.

YVONNE
Not really in the mood for tonight, Steven's parents have to pick him up early anyway. But have fun!
EMMY
boooooo, you whore.

Lindsey frowned. "Really? Shit."

Without another word, she promptly headed over to the side table where several small pieces of paper were stacked and began shuffling through them, presumably to sort out any oddball dares, truths, or extra numbers for her meticulously planned games.

Xander stood off behind one of the couches, talking to a friend. Violet took notice, but continued scanning the room. To the right, at the back wall of the basement, a set of shutter-style doors divided the entertainment area from a storage space. She eyed the doors with pursed lips before slowly scanning the room. She knew almost everyone here, though not well. There were somewhere between thirty and forty people crammed into the basement. She wondered briefly if she'd find herself in that closet with anyone before the night's end, and if Xander might be that one.

"Alright, everyone, circle up!" Lindsey called in the classical sing-songy voice of an over-dramatic theatre kid, and the conversations settled to a dull mumbling as everyone prepared for the rules.

"You all know the drill," she continued. "I have three hats, up here full of truths and dares. One has all the truths, one has mild dares, and this one," she shook a black beanie covered in a flame design (definitely Travis's), "has our spicier dares." She raised her eyebrows twice, punctuating the gesture with a quick wink. "You have the right to reject the truth or dare and replace it with another at any time, or you can pass it to another player by winning a three finger round of Never Have I Ever. Everyone understand?"

A chorus of yeses and nods replied. Violet chose to sit opposite of Xander, and nestled herself on the floor between Emmy and a boy, Tanner. She'd had a history class with him freshman year, but she didn't know a whole lot about him. Certainly they'd be a little more familiar after this evening.

"Who's going first?" Lindsey asked, shaking her hats once more.

Emmy was prepared, hopping up to swipe the flamed hat in front of her in the blink of an eye. She dug around inside the hat before settling on a neatly folded sheet of paper inside. She unwrapped it, building the anticipation. Her eyes squinted at the tiny sheet. "The Blindfolded Butt Grab. Find four volunteers who are willing to get groped. Try to identify who is who by only grabbing their butt." The circle snickered as Emmy happily turned to Lindsey. "Do I get to pick the butts!?"

"No!" Lindsey reached behind her, pulling a sleep mask from her purse and tossed it at Emmy. "Put that on."

Emmy did as she was instructed as Lindsey gathered up some butts to grope. Two gentlemen and two ladies lined up quietly while Lindsey's friend

Delia spun Emmy around a few times, guiding her to the neatly organized row of eight buttcheeks.

Emmy wasted no time; she took both hands and grabbed a thick handful in each, lifting and jiggling right, left, right left, until she felt satisfied and moved to the next. The crowd let out minor snorts, but most tried to remain quiet as they looked on the moment.

On the third grab, she gripped and released immediately. "Oh, that's Ryan." The room erupted in laughter.

Lindsey held back a laugh, "But how do you know?"

"I'd know that tiny little apple bottom anywhere!"

An excellent start to the evening, certainly, but it wouldn't stop there. The pile which collected the pulled strips of paper grew until it toppled over with hits such as "take a body shot of ketchup off the person to your right", "text your ex saying you miss them", and "who here would you skinny dip with?"

Violet was a mild dare kind of girl, but on the last round, with options limited to choosing to select a strip from the flaming hat, or a truth for the third round in a row.

"Come on," Emmy whispered, "Just one."

Violet's chest tightened as she eyed the beanie. She glanced up and met eyes with Xander across the circle, intrigued by the potential of her next move. She wondered what she was so afraid of. Surely nothing in that hat could be worse than anything she'd already done with Xander.

She reached in quickly and pulled the first one her fingers touched, returning her hands to her chest as if there was a chance no one saw her pull. She stared intently at the sheet as she unfolded it, tracing the lines of each word with her eyes.

"Take the person to your right into the closet with you. You have two minutes to come up with and name a brand new sex position."

Violet blushed and she met eyes with Tanner as some of the guys cackled and clapped at the idea.

"Alright, go on!" Lindsey said, unlocking the storage door and motioning inside. "Timer starts when the door closes!"

Violet let out a deep breath and rose to her feet. Tanner followed as well. Neither had said a word to each other.

Once the door closed, and the only light came from the slats on the door, they looked at each other uncomfortably.

Tanner chuckled a little. "So, what kind of position you thinking?"

Violet smiled uncomfortably, crossing her arms. "Um, I don't know. Can you, like, do anything cool?"

Tanner scratched his neck a little. "I used to be able to stand on my head?"

Violet's arms dropped and her smile widened a bit. "Okay, um," she paused, looking at an empty plot of carpet beside them, "could you…?" She trailed off.

"Yeah, I can try." He squatted and thought for a moment. "I'm going to do it against the wall."

Violet nodded, "Yeah, yeah. That's probably best." She followed him to the wall as she carefully balanced himself up against the unfinished concrete.

"Okay," he huffed, clearly uncomfortable with his own weight now on his neck. "Now what?"

Violet looked at him with a cocked head. "Maybe, just… open your legs a bit, and I could sort of…" she thought out loud.

Tanner spread his legs and Violet started to reach forward before she stopped herself, returning her hands to her chest. "What?" he asked,

Violet's lips twitched, "I don't know, it's just a little uncomfortable." She let out a nervous laugh.

"It's cool, just do what you gotta do."

Tanner's sweatpants laid neatly. She noticed the bulge between his legs, strategically reached forward just above, but not touching. "We would make it like a handy situation?" She offered, miming a stroke in an up and down manner.

Tanner let out a labored laugh, and flopped himself off to the side, landing on his knees. "Like churning butter?" He smiled genuinely at Violet, and she laughed right back.

"Yeah, I guess that's what we'll have to call it." And together they reached back for the door. Show time.

CHAPTER SIXTEEN

A red hot flush swept across Violet's cheeks as Tanner exited the closet in front of her. He rotated his shoulders back a few times and made a show of cracking his knuckles. He seemed surprisingly confident when met by the gaze of an anticipating audience.

The room quieted as he sauntered to the wall opposite the closet and bent over, steadying himself to stand on his head with his back to the cool plaster.

Violet could only hope she looked that confident because she felt like a puppy reluctantly obeying its owner as she followed. She wondered if maybe his confidence only came from looking like a stud in front of his friends. Yet, as she watched him set himself for their raunchy tableau, she noticed that he didn't necessarily seem like a "stud".

His hair was just slightly too long as it hung in front of his eyes. They were a light caramel brown, and evidently only visible as his bangs laid against the ground. He wasn't particularly fit, his lips were somewhat thin, and his nose was slightly crooked. By any definition of the word, he was fairly average looking.

Thankfully, by this point, his face looked just as red as hers, though presumably that came from the blood rushing to his head and not the anxiety of feigning a handy in front of a group of friends.

She reached two hands out and wrapped them into fists, one on top of another, and began to churn. She avoided any eye contact by staring straight at the wall above her adoring crowd as they hooted and hollered.

"Oh my *god!*" Lindsey snorted.

"What's the name!?" Emmy's words called over a chorus of uproarious conversations and hysterical laughter.

Violet finally took her eyes off the wall and began to crack a smile at the ridiculousness of it all. "Churning the butter," she stated as though it was obvious.

When another roar of laughs hit her ears, she couldn't help but start giggling along with them. As Tanner's leg lowered and Violet's arms receded to her sides, she felt an overwhelming sense of relief. It wasn't so bad in hindsight, especially now that it was over. The boys doled out high-fives, Violet noticed Xander gave Tanner a good pat on the back, while the girls shook their heads and rolled their eyes as though they didn't also enjoy a good, hearty laugh as a result of the performance. She felt a surge of adrenaline from the attention. It was almost powerful.

The games eventually ended and their numbers grew smaller, but Violet's energy was still riding on that subtle high. Lindsey pulled blankets off stacks resting behind the couch and tossed them one by one to each person who announced they would be staying.

"Xander?" she called, eying him from across the room.

"Nah, I think I'll just walk home in a bit," he replied from his perch in a chair in the corner of the room.

"Okay, Tanner?" She moved right along.

"Yup," he replied automatically and a soft blanket flew by Violet's face before Tanner scooped it into his arms.

"Vi?"

Violet replied in the affirmative and only had time to blink once before a large, apparently hand-knitted afghan flew straight into her face. She pulled it to her lap, feeling each of the large pills and individual stitches scrape across her skin and inhaling a big, musty whiff of what she could only assume were moth balls and grandma sweat. She wrinkled her nose while her eyes flitted over to the furry texture inches away, resting between Tanner's arms.

She gave a half-hearted smile, knowing the answer before she asked, "Any chance you'd want to trade?"

Tanner glanced at her lap and back to her eyes, breathed a laugh and spoke, "I can smell it from here, no thank you."

Violet gave a face. Yeah, that figured.

"But," Tanner wasn't finished, "We can share if you want?" He offered the question innocently.

"Absolutely!" she replied without a moment's hesitation, closing the distance between them and leaving the scratchy afghan in her place. She looked out the corner of her eye to where Xander sat, but he still sat, stoic and unreadable.

Soon, he gave up his chair to leave the party, walking past Violet and Tanner, chatting in their little corner. His spot was soon filled by Travis who kicked the foot-rest out of the chair and called Lindsey over to his lap, where she came, wrapped in a blanket and ready for bed after a long night of playing hostess.

Each probable sleeping location filled quickly, leaving only squares of carpet in the center of the room to lie. Tanner glanced around the room, hoping to find a better alternative.

"There's a futon in the closet that you can pull out if you want," Travis noted over Lindsey's head and she laid curled on top of him, apparently texting.

Tanner and Violet's necks snapped to look at each other.

"Um... sure," Violet spoke, answering a question that hadn't been asked.

They rose from the ground and paced the room from their corner to the closet door. She had noticed the futon while they were in there. She wondered how many rounds of Seven-Minutes-in-Heaven were spent on that same, thin mattress. It really did appear more like a sack, making the whole experience feel slightly more shady as she climbed on top, crossing her legs as Tanner sat beside her. They both eyed the closet door, still open.

"Do you… want to close the door?" Tanner asked.

"It doesn't matter," she replied. It mattered a little.

Tanner didn't rise to close it, just shuffled himself further along the futon so he was positioned on the far side. Violet laid beside him, leaving a space of about six inches between them. She stared at the slightly open door, listening to the muffled whispers of individual conversations happening on the other side before turning and facing Tanner.

They both appeared to hold their breath, afraid to see who would make the next move.

And with the last bit of energy she held, Violet closed the gap between them and laid her head in the crook of Tanner's arm and head. It was warm, and surprisingly comfortable. It didn't take long to fall asleep.

*   *   *

"I'm still surprised they're not up yet," a conversation echoed quietly through the open closet door.

Violet kept her eyes shut, not yet willing to deal with the sunlight poking its rays through the tiny basement windows. Her cheek felt warm as she realized it was still pressed against Tanner's upper arm. Did they sleep like this all night?

"I wonder what Xander will say?" The unmistakable voice of Lindsey questioned slightly too loud, like she was expecting a chuckle or some sort of reaction. Violet only heard some low breaths in reply.

"I don't think they're official," another voice responded. Emmy's.

"I'm surprised. She doesn't seem like the type," an unrecognizable voice whispered.

"Do you think they did anything last night?" Lindsey continued.

"Please. Violet? She'd never." Emmy defended.

A scoff broke the quiet of the conversation. "I'm not convinced. No one thought she'd be hooking up with her ex on the down-low either. She's clearly full of surprises." The unfamiliar voice teased.

Violet finally opened her eyes. She noticed she was smiling a little. She'd never considered her reputation to be as fun and mysterious as the party-goers seemed to reveal. She couldn't help but smirk at the comment. She noticed Tanner's position had shifted. His face was turned to the wall, and his mouth hung open as his breath came out slow and deep. Sleep still had its hold on him.

Violet moved her arms first and lifted her body straight up, moving slowly and deliberately so not to wake him. She stretched her legs over the edge of the futon and heard a slight creak, which silenced the crowd outside the door promptly.

She stretched her arms back as she stepped to the door, still open from the night before. "Morning!" she called. The small group smiled inconspicuously and greeted her as though she hadn't been the topic of their conversation only moments before. *Too bad*, she thought. She wanted to hear what else they had to say about her.

It wasn't long before Violet and Emmy said their goodbyes and set off to find Violet's car parked along the side of the road. The drive was fraught with groans from Emmy as she sent reassuring texts to her mother that she was already on the way and definitely wouldn't miss whatever silly soccer game / concert / karate tournament her siblings had that afternoon. She ungracefully pulled a pair of sweatpants over her shorts from the night before and threw a hoodie over her tank top to give the impression of a good, innocent, girl's night before hastily exiting the vehicle and throwing half-hearted "Text you soon!" in Violet's direction (all the while tripping over her too-long sweats up the driveway.)

Classic Emmy.

Upon reaching home, she wandered through the mess of the garage, questioning if somehow, it had gotten even more disorganized. She noticed an open box with holiday decorations strewn about, a little bit of everything it seemed. A black cat hissed beside a Santa with a huge 3D bag of gifts, while a deflated turkey acting as a tarp, corralling everything along with lights of various colors and sizes. Mr. Gray must have been attempting to decorate, but the nakedness of the house seemed to imply he'd given up.

"Hey, Dad, I'm home!" Violet called, dropping her bag in the laundry room off the garage entrance and heading swiftly upstairs, leaving no part of her to hear her father's reply, except maybe the wind off her heels.

Violet plopped on her bed, yanking her sandals off and tossing them in the corner of the room, she'd put them away later. Her bra shortly followed them.

Over at her desk, she opened her laptop and swiped the mouse pad to reveal the *Cosmo* homepage still open. Her eyes flitted to the article advertised in the lower right corner "The 15 Best Masturbation Scenes You Can Stream Right Now."

She made a face of distaste, but it dropped as she considered it. She'd never really thought about it before. She glanced at the time then over to her slightly cracked door. She grabbed at the waistband of her pants, sitting down and mousing to the address bar on her screen, before stopping suddenly, frozen in thought. She'd decided. Not now. Maybe sometime soon, if she was in the mood. Though, she couldn't imagine the "mood" ever coming.

Instead, she distracted herself by deleting the N-E-T she'd started typing for Netflix, and replaced them with F-A-C, tapping enter when it auto-filled to her distraction: Facebook.

She began scrolling. At the top of the feed was a post from Yvonne. A vague status in which the only content was a single smiley face. *Good for her*, the bland statement echoed in the back of her mind as she continued scrolling, stopping on a post from Jess.

Jess Daniels Principal Mick is outright REFUSING to allow a Gay-Straight Alliance in our school, citing "controversiality" as the reason! This blatant disrespect and disregard for our LGBTQIAA+ students is despicable and I will be taking this as far as it needs to go. This BULLYING and ISOLATION must STOP.

Beneath the words sat the link to Yvonne's article. Violet scrolled past the link and immediately clicked into the comments.

Shawn Seymour You said it Jess! Let me know how I can help!

Jess Daniels I definitely will! I have some stuff in the works.

Zac King Mick is traaasssssshhhhhhhh.

Dani Chase we should start a petition... this is ridiculous!

Jess Daniels Agreed! I'm already working on it!

Angel Wright Thank you for everything you're doing to protect the LGBT community-- you're a true ally!

Jess Daniels <3

Alice Daniels Proud of you baby!!! xoxo Grandma Alice

Devonte Smith what??? how can he just say no!?

Dani Chase power trip, probably! he's barely been the principal for 2 years and the schools already gone to hell!

Jess Daniels He claims he's "doing what's best" for the school, but he provided absolutely no significant reason outside of "avoiding controversy".

Zac King lol. So hes just homophobic? got it.

Violet sighed and leaned back in her chair. What was there to say that the comments hadn't already covered? After wrestling with the words for a few minutes, she stopped typing and retyping and settled on a simple click.

Violet Gray liked this status.

CHAPTER SEVENTEEN

Did the students always seem to talk so much before? The hallways buzzed with rumors about everything from Jess's Facebook blow-up, to Lindsey's party, who made out with who, and which students ended up in the police blotter.

"I heard they faked a kidnapping, is it true?" Violet's eyes were wide with curiosity.

"They didn't fake it. Kaelin said they were all hanging out in Mia's basement and I guess Ollie found her dad's toolbox and she wanted to see if she could break the duct tape if they wrapped it around her wrists, like in all those self-defense videos on YouTube, you know?" Emmy replied as she chewed on a thick piece of pink bubblegum with a yellow hall-pass curling around itself in her palms. She should have been in class, but of course she needed a "restroom break" during Violet and Yvonne's lunch period.

Yvonne had been notably absent from lunch, citing that she needed to do an interview for her next newspaper article, and Violet was itching to discuss all of the wild news making its way around the school.

"And what, she just couldn't?" Violet inquired.

"No," Emmy continued, leaning toward Violet to add the illusion of secrecy to their storytelling, as though this tale wasn't already being discussed at each of the surrounding tables. There was no time to waste with something this interesting, hence her increasingly bent hall-pass which continued to crumble inside her fists.

"Ollie and Drew started just wrapping her wrists and then she *let* them wrap up her ankles and tape her mouth too. I guess to see if she could get out of all of it, or something? And then they just all decided they were hungry, threw Mia, still totally duct taped over their shoulders and carried her out to the car in broad daylight!"

"So the neighbor saw and called the cops!?"

"Yup," Emmy smirked. "They ran the plates in their system or whatever and found out it was Drew's dad's, so they showed up at his house all serious and his parents had no idea! When they finally found the car, Mia was out of the duct tape and they were all just hanging out at the skate park. They brought everyone in for questioning and they made everyone's parents come to pick them up, it was *wild.* Kaelin said Mia's parents aren't letting them over ever again."

"Fair enough," Violet shook her head, bewildered. "How hungry do you have to be to just leave with your friend still in duct tape handcuffs?" She couldn't help but crack a smile at how comical it all was, since it really wasn't all that serious in the end.

"Anyway," Emmy changed the topic, "I meant to ask on Sunday, but I totally forgot after Luis' soccer game, have you talked to Xander?"

Violet's nose twitched. "No, not really," she attempted to make it sound less serious. She'd kind of let that part of the conversation she'd eavesdropped on whisk over her head. Violet and Xander weren't a real couple, they'd already had this discussion. She'd already been on that date with Derek with his blessing. Why should he care if she slept in the same bed with another guy? Especially when nothing happened. She hadn't even so much as kissed anyone that night.

"You didn't, like, do anything with Tanner on the futon, right?" Emmy asked.

"What? No. We just slept. It was really more about the blanket than him," Violet confessed, still uncertain about the whole thing. "Why?"

"I don't know, Lindsey was saying some stuff, but you know, she's kind of a drama queen. Whatever. I'm just saying, Tanner's a nice guy and all, but you can get someone way hotter. You still have Steven's friend's number, right?"

Violet nodded with her eyes turned, glancing over the heads in the cafeteria, and landing on a patch of plain white wall near the ceiling as she chewed contemplatively on a carrot stick. *At least I knew what to talk about with Tanner.*

*   *   *

Violet fast-walked through the hallway, skidding to a stop in front of her locker and frantically twisting the knob to the combination.

"Hey," a voice broke through the dull roar of the hallway a little too loudly in her ear.

She jumped and the top book of the three in her arms slid off the stack to the floor with a loud crack.

"Shoot," she groaned, squatting to grab it.

"I've got it." It was Tanner. He bent over and pulled the book up, setting it back on Violet's stack. "Sorry," he said, "I didn't mean to scare you."

"It's fine," she laughed, pulling the trigger to swing open the narrow metal door and began piling her books inside. "I'm just always rushing to switch out books and I guess I was just hyper-focused on the combination. I wasn't expecting it is all."

"Why the rush?" Tanner inquired.

Violet couldn't help but take the bait to complain about her locker. She only ever had the time to visit it first thing in the morning and at the very end of the day. If she really rushed, she could trade books right after lunch so she didn't have to carry all of her books to every class, but it always cut close. "None of my classes are anywhere near my locker. This is the only time I'm close enough to it to swap them out during the day."

"Oof," he groaned. "That sucks. It's already seventh period."

"Right. And apparently I can't switch it for something closer because all the lockers in the West Hall upstairs are being used."

"Damn, well, you know," he started, "my locker is up in the West Hall. If you need, I can give you the combination and you can keep your books in there. All of my stuff fits on the top shelf so I don't really use the rest of it."

"Really?" Violet smiled, slamming the metal door so the row of lockers rattled and vibrated in response to the clang of the metal.

"Sure! Um," he looked down in his pocket and pulled out a pen, quickly scribbling on the back of a notebook Violet had just supplied to her stack. "That's my number. Just text me at the end of the day and I can give you the combination and stuff. I don't actually know the number offhand," his words rolling one into another, clearly sensing Violet's rush.

"You're awesome, thank you so much!" and Violet took off down the hall. She didn't quite make it to class on time, but she felt good all the same.

Spanish ran smoothly. She wrote out conjugations and spoke absent-mindedly with her classmates in a language close to Spanglish until the bell finally rang, meaning she could finally head to her chemistry class and push through the last bell of the day with her friends.

She poked her head into the classroom to find it mostly empty as the majority of their class loitered about the hallway. Yvonne stood by her desk in the corner, pulling her books out for class while Ms. Elliot wrote terms on the board. Emmy hadn't yet made her appearance for class. She often wandered in at the last minute.

"Hey!" Violet called, doing a brisk walk to her friend. "We missed you at lunch. How's the article going?"

Yvonne didn't look up from her bag as she zipped it up. "Good." Her reply was curt and dismissive.

"Are you okay?" Violet's head cocked to one side, her brows furrowing to a look of confusion and concern.

"Mhm," Yvonne nodded once, plopping in her chair quickly. Still refusing to make eye contact.

"Are you sure? Did something happen? You seem kind of… off." Violet slowly lowered her books to the desk and sat beside her.

Her eyes rolled. "Really?" She turned her neck only, keeping her body forward facing as she spoke. "I heard about the party, Violet. I should be the one asking you what happened." She returned her attention to her book, flipping through the pages until she found something recognizable.

"What do you mean?" Violet's voice was exasperated. "Nothing happened."

"So you didn't sleep with Tanner McBride in a closet all night? Or ignore Xander all night? Oh, and what about Derek?" She stopped to groan. "I can't even keep up with all of your boyfriends anymore," she mumbled passively.

"Are you serious?" She didn't even know how to respond. Her hands were shaking, and she felt a lump forming in her throat. "You know they're not boyfriends, I'm just…" she struggled to think of the word, "Dating around." She felt those final words come out a little too quietly. What was she making such a big deal out of this for? She thought Yvonne understood Xander was just a friend. She went out with Derek as a favor to her and they didn't click. She couldn't possibly be expecting Violet to keep dating Derek just so she could see Steven during the week, could she? That's ridiculous.

Yvonne scoffed in a low breath. "Whatever. You're blowing off a nice guy to blow whatever dude is in front of you."

Violet's face felt hot. It was past red; it was white with a tension in her jaw as she attempted to swallow her anger. Is that what people were saying? It seemed so different from what she'd heard on Sunday morning. "Those rumors are stupid," she hissed impulsively, "I don't care about them, so why do you?"

She did care. She cared quite a lot, but she'd decided long before this conversation that she'd rather face the scrutiny over her broken hymen for a few weeks than be the virgin girl forever.

Even if she hadn't, there was no going back now.

Yvonne finally turned her whole body to face Violet, and her voice growled "You don't *care*!? I--" she cut herself off, and grimaced, tucking her tongue between her top lip and teeth, sucking in so the veins in her neck showed prominently. "Of course you don't," her words were matter-of-fact. Violet held her breath. "If you really cared about them, you'd stop acting like such a slut."

The room blurred. The mixture of a sudden wave of salty tears flooding the corners of her eyes and the sheer speed with which she left the room was undoubtedly the cause. She'd stormed out the doorway too quickly to pay any attention to who might have heard Yvonne, and she slid through the hallways so quickly she couldn't tell who may have noticed her crying.

She pushed past the two girls leaving the bathroom without a second thought, and slammed the first stall door shut, breaking down completely before she'd even managed to lock it.

CHAPTER EIGHTEEN

Small, weak sobs exhaled from Violet's lips. Each one punctuated by a shaky inhale as she attempted to process what had happened.

Yvonne had always been a good friend to her. All anyone ever talked about at this school was their sex-lives. How could she have possibly turned on her for just doing what everyone else did? Not to mention how rarely she actually discussed it.

Maybe that was it.

Violet never considered until that moment that maybe the issue was how her friends were hearing her news through the grapevine and not from the source.

She croaked out another sob. She couldn't even imagine how to begin to have that conversation, at least not without somehow affecting Xander.

Fake It till You Make It

Yeah, I had sex with Xander but it wasn't particularly great, but I kept doing it anyway. It sounded worse when she tried to put it into words.

She felt herself tripping over some way to make it sound right, or to justify her own actions to herself. It felt like she was conducting her own critical interview in her head, like a celebrity being blindsided on a talk show with a topic they insisted they wouldn't discuss.

Why even bother?

I thought we were doing something wrong; it was only our first time.

But you kept it going for weeks? You had to have done it more than once.

Well, after a while… I thought maybe it was just me.

What if it's Xander?

Even if it is, I can't just tell my friends that. What if it gets back to him?

So you don't trust them not to tell?

No, I do! Just… news spreads quickly.

But what if it's you?

Violet gulped at the thought. She'd danced around it so many times, circumventing the isolation that went with it, but in that moment the walls of the stall seemed to close in.

It's you. You're the weird one. That's why nothing's working out right, that's why you don't get it. You're broken. You're a slut. You're a sad, broken, slut.

She felt a throbbing in her temples. Her tears had exhausted her fully, leaving unguarded holes for these invasive, negative thoughts to snake around her brain and squeeze so tightly, she'd eventually lose feeling and go numb. She was already feeling weak without this barrage of targeted attacks against her insecurities.

She inhaled with hopes of steadying her breathing. Her hand hovered over the stall lock. She couldn't just sit there and beat herself up, she'd return to class with her head held high and act like nothing happened. She could surely manage that.

The stall door swung open to reveal her tear-stained cheeks in the adjacent mirror. Her entire face was red and splotchy. Her under-eyes swelled as if there was an unlimited store of tears preparing to be squeezed out of them like water from a balloon.

Fake It till You Make It

She took another deep breath, this time with only one shake near the end. Now the air itself seemed to be pressing in on her. It was somehow worse than the cool metallic walls of the stall. The air was hot and sticky—almost suffocating.

Violet sniffed. Her reflection followed as they approached one another. Her gray eyes met those of the smudged reflection as she forced a half-hearted smile.

Just fake it. You can make it until the end of the day. Her smile widened just a hair at the silly rhyme. *Fake it till you make it.*

Her breaths felt more even now, though her eyes still looked bloodshot. It would take a while for that to go back to normal, she knew. So she threw her hair back over her shoulders, smoothed a stray hair from flying away from the crown of her head and turned briskly to head back to her classroom.

The door was closed, but Violet's posture immediately straightened. If she was going to have to walk through the classroom and head back to her seat beside Yvonne, she'd need to have all the false confidence her body could muster.

She knocked three times and waited with a tension building in her shoulders.

You're not a slut.

Yvonne is wrong.

You're not weird.

You're not broken.

You're not.

The door opened slightly to reveal Ms. Elliot's rounded face, peaking around the crack in the door as the sun crested the horizon.

"Violet," she spoke softly. Her eyes seemed to take in the same details Violet had in the mirror of the girl's bathroom. "Why don't you head down to the nurse? I'll send someone with your things in a little bit." Her smile was laced with trace amounts of concern, and perhaps a pinch of pity, but in that moment Violet's train of thought adjusted.

You're not trapped.

You're free.

You can deal with this later.

And the prospect of putting everything off until later was just too irresistible

"Okay."

Without another word, Violet fast-walked her way to the nearest staircase, just slow enough that it wouldn't look suspicious, but just fast enough that it felt like the glorious escape it was.

The open doorways dabbled her walk down to the main hallway with white noise and the occasional, yet unmistakable call of class clowns and rowdy groups of troublemakers anxiously awaiting the end of the day.

Violet's arms crossed in front of her body as if she was attempting to shield herself from harm, although the damage was done. Her phone still sat in the classroom, and she suddenly wished she had it, just to distract herself from the cloud of self-hatred surrounding her.

As she rounded the corner into the main hallway, a hand gripped her shoulder. She jumped and twisted to see Xander with a crease between his eyebrows, looking her directly in the eye.

She'd been so absorbed in her own thoughts, she must not have realized he'd been just behind her. She wanted to ask why he wasn't in class, but his question came first.

"Are you okay?" His voice always seemed so monotonous to her, but in this moment he sounded so sincere, and all it took was the thought of answering that question for the dam to break, causing her eyes to once again flood with tears.

She couldn't see. Her vision was blurred in waves of salt water, but she couldn't feel his arms wrap around her as she fell into his chest and began soaking the center of his shirt.

As the two damp spots beneath each eye merged to form one large stain, Xander reached an arm around Violet's shoulders and began walking with her back the way they came, through a set of wide open double doors and beneath a staircase where she could sob in relative privacy.

Xander said nothing, just rubbed along her arm and let her crying exhaust her more. The sniffles and shakes took their time slowing down.

"I'm sorry," Violet whimpered, the words wavering slightly as she again tried to steady her breathing.

"Want to talk about it?" Xander finally asked.

The pause in speech was scarcely silent as Violet attempted to even out her voice enough to speak. She didn't want to talk about Yvonne, but there was a question sitting at the tip of her tongue, ready to roll off.

"Are you mad at me?" The question felt infantile. Instead of a smooth slide off her tongue, it felt more like an off-balance somersault performed by a toddler.

To her pleasant surprise, he answered quickly. "No. Why would I be?"

"I mean," Violet choked, "I know we had this... thing going on, but everyone seems to think I'm a slut because we slept together and we're not spending all this time together."

"Who's everyone?" he asked with a twinge of true curiosity.

She sighed. "Yvonne apparently."

"Well," Xander shrugged. "Sounds like she had a big bowl of bitch-flakes this morning and she needs to relax." Violet hated herself for smiling a little at the comment. "She obviously needs to get laid and she's taking it out of you."

She didn't necessarily agree with that sentiment, but it certainly helped to have someone on her side in the matter. There was another lull in their conversation. They both sat with their backs against the wall as Violet completely calmed herself, drying the remaining wet spots near the bridge of her nose. For a moment, she considered what a shame it was that the connection between her and Xander didn't seem to be romantic at all. In spite of all they had done, it didn't feel particularly sexual either. It was a pure, genuine platonic friendship, and this exchange had made that abundantly clear that the "benefits" in this friendship were extraneous at best.

"I think we should stop," Violet announced with the most even voice she'd managed since her fit had begun.

Xander nodded. "Yeah."

"No regrets though?" she asked.

"None," Xander replied with a smile. Violet felt relieved. Something about the official end of their intimate relationship made her feel like a weight had been lifted off her shoulders.

"Is it going to be weird now?" Her next question came in a joking tone.

He chuckled in response. "No weirder than usual."

"Fair enough." She sighed a soft laugh and leaned her head back against the wall.

The light steps of tennis shoes came squeaking from above as a student came galloping down the staircase. Xander and Violet peaked around the corner from their hiding place to see Emmy bounding off toward the nurse's office with Violet's bag.

"Hey!" Violet called and Emmy stopped and turned, recognizing the call and heading back in their direction.

"Hey," she said, glancing from Violet to Xander, and back again. "Are you good? Yvonne seems really pissed."

Violet scoffed and stood up to collect her bag from Emmy. "Yeah, well, let her be." Her tone was sharp and acidic. She quickly pulled her phone out of the front pocket to see if Tanner had replied to the text she sent during Spanish.

VIOLET

Hey, it's Violet :)

It looked as though Tanner had replied right at the beginning of eighth period after Violet abandoned her phone to cry in the classroom.

TANNER
Hey! I just checked the number, its 2768. Combo is 15 07 34

"You wanna tell me what happened?" Emmy's voice interrupted Violet's train of thought.

Violet looked up from her phone. As much as she was sure Emmy wouldn't side with Yvonne in this particular argument, she really wasn't in the mood to find out.

"No," she said, "I'm going to move my books to my new locker."

Emmy didn't object, just nodded with a glint of disappointment in her eyes.

"Want me to help?" Xander offered.

"No," she said again. "I'll see you both later."

And she turned on her heels and headed off to her inconveniently placed locker. She had just enough time to get her things moved into Tanner's locker before the final bell rang.

CHAPTER NINETEEN

The week moved slowly, or at least it felt that way. Every morning Violet found herself running later and later so she wouldn't have to face Yvonne before first period.

EMMY

She says you changed, but she also said shes upset you didn't give Derek a shot. I think its just a misunderstanding, you just need to talk.

VIOLET

I'll talk when she apologizes.

Violet knew Yvonne. She wasn't the type to apologize, she always thought she was right. To be fair, she usually was, but that was in academic matters, not necessarily social situations. Still, part of her expected her friend to recognize their friendship was more important than a petty argument. Violet certainly believed it was, but her pride was too bruised to make the first move.

In math class, Violet went about business as usual with Xander and Travis. Truly, it was as though nothing changed, and interestingly enough, Travis seemed to have more juicy gossip about Xander and Violet's relationship than even they had.

"Did you hear Violet cheated on you, Xan?" he offered nonchalantly, folding a sheet of notebook paper into a tiny triangular football.

"What?" both Xander and Violet replied, only milliseconds from being in unison.

"Yeah. Linds and her friends were talking about it. Apparently Ariana heard from Kinsey, who heard from Bridget, who heard from her uncle's cousin's dog's neighbor that you were in the hallway on Monday crying because Xander found out."

Travis and Lindsey really were perfect for each other; they both *loved* to stir the pot and see what happened.

"And you were begging for him to take you back which, apparently…" he glanced up at the two of them sitting shoulder to shoulder on the opposite side of his desk, "he agreed to."

After a short, uncomfortable pause, Violet let out a loud snort. It was all just so absurd! How could anyone just make up such a blatant lie and speak it as the truth?

"I don't know when everyone got so obsessed with my business," she said. The words sounded like a joke, but Violet felt as though they held a profound truth to them.

"Tell them we broke up," Xander spoke, leaning his chair back slightly with his fingers out as a goal post for Travis's paper football.

Violet said no words, just turned briskly and gave him an inquisitive stare.

"Steer into the skid," he shrugged. "Maybe they'll leave it alone."

It honestly wasn't such a bad idea. What's one more lie in a mix of half-truths and misinformation anyway?

By the time lunch came around, Violet skipped out on the usual lunch room at the usual table with Yvonne to go and meet Jess in the library during her study hall.

Jess sat at a row of computer screens lining the back wall, leaving one seat conveniently open for Violet to slip in beside her. Her braids draped down her back to her waist; she'd recently added an array of pastel rainbow colors throughout her hair. They stood out brightly against her dark locks, making her easy to spot.

"Hey, what's going on?" Violet asked, noticing the deep focus Jess held on her screen. Her eyes moved gently from side-to-side, squinting slightly, reading and rereading a document which so aggressively gripped her attention.

"I'm drafting a letter to go alongside the petition for the GSA. I have almost two-hundred signatures, and I want to get it to Principal Mick as soon as possible," she spoke without looking at Violet, who had signed her petition that Tuesday when she first started eating her lunch discretely from her bag in the library.

Principal Mick had yet to make any comment on the article in the school paper, but Jess had speculated all week that he would be making some sort of counter-move to excuse his actions and distract from the "negative press". Violet couldn't help but admire what an amazing and dedicated politician she would make one day.

"Need any help?" Violet offered, shoving a ripped corner piece of a sandwich into her cheek quickly.

"Not yet. Maybe when I finish," she added, beginning to type aggressively on the outdated, mechanical keyboard.

The period went quickly. Once Violet had finished her lunch, she actually had time to work on homework assignments.

When the bell rang, she called a goodbye to Jess, leaving her to hastily pack her bag and log out of the computer simultaneously. Violet followed a path to the West Hall and approached her new locker with a smile. While she didn't really see Tanner at their shared locker all too often, she did sort of enjoy having a locker roommate. In the middle of the day, she decided to leave him a thank you note resting on top of his books on the shelf.

TANNER,

Thanks again for letting me share your locker!

You're the best!

Hope you're having a good day!

xo Vi

She remembered feeling saucy as she scribbled in that little "xo." She wondered if he'd read into it as much as she thought about it before she wrote it in. It didn't matter though, because writing notes to each other once or twice a day had become their fun little game whenever they were bored in class.

Vi,

I am having a good day! Just bored in American history. Mr. Newman added his birthday to the list of important historical events, which is next week coincidentally.. I think he's fishing for gifts, haha!

Hope you're day is going well too!

−T.

Violet recalled rolling her eyes at the misused "you're" in the final sentence, and made sure to tease him for it in her brief response scribbled on a sticky note and slapped on his initial response.

T,

you_R_* :)

xo V

By the time Violet reached their locker, she twisted the lock, popped it off and stretched the metal mouth of the locker wider, looking to see if there was a new response waiting for her.

There was.

Her fingers wrapped around the paper, folded into eighths and resting at eye level on the folded edges so her name was visible. She unfolded once, twice, three times until the letter was exposed.

V,

Are you doing anything tonight?

Having a bad movie night with a few friends around 7.

Text if you need the address.

If not, I'll see you Monday!

-T.

As she read the note, Violet's stomach did a flip. She imagined how it might have felt if she were the one who'd written it. Was this a sort of date? Or was she overthinking it? That last line sure made it seem like he was playing this off as a casual thing. Maybe it was a casual thing? Maybe he's just being nice? Or maybe he put himself out there because he's interested?

Was she interested in dating Tanner for real?

She shook the questions out of her head like a dog shaking after bath and closed the locker door. With her bag a bit lighter, she scurried through the crowds of the hallway to her art class where she could think about it after the bell rang.

She sat at her stool just in time as her teacher shuffled around the room, depositing the sketchbooks he'd collected the day before.

He stood at the front of the class and said, "Today, we're going to practice drawing from references. I'd like you all to search for images of bicycles. I chose this subject because, in my experience, it's impossible to draw one correctly without looking at a reference."

As he spoke, the projector behind him flipped through a series of bicycle drawings in charcoal and graphite looking wonky and off in one way or another, eliciting a few laughs from the class.

"See what you can get done today, focus on shape and light. I want to see some accurate shadows today."

The silence of the class dissolved into a low buzzing of whispers like white noise and laughs while the students searched for reference images.

Violet pulled her phone from the front pocket of her bag and went to click into a Google search before stopping slowly and moving her finger over her Messages app.

The screen filled with the messages between her and Emmy from earlier. She backed out quickly and scrolled not too far to find her message chain with Tanner.

VIOLET

I'm definitely down to watch a bad movie!

The reply came quickly.

TANNER

Sweet! Address is 728 Jefferson Court.

VIOLET

Noted. Also, why is it a bad movie? Is your taste just that terrible? :P

TANNER

Just come ready to laugh :)

Violet caught herself smiling as she backed out of the messages and returned her attention to the assignment.

Draw a bike.

She glanced around at the other students at her table, all with bikes of different shapes and colors, mountain bikes, cruisers, some with baskets, some with bells and tassels.

"This is the same bike I had when I first learned to ride," she overheard a girl from the table next to her speak, slightly over the rumble of the noise.

Violet held her phone with both hands, thumbs poised to make their move on the keyboard.

She cocked her head to one side as letters filled the search bar.

The screen flooded with images of tandem bikes with two seats. Something about a single rider bike seemed too simple, and she was up for the challenge.

CHAPTER TWENTY

The night fell quickly, hastened by the dark gray clouds which blocked out the remaining rays of light from the sun. Violet grabbed a thicker jacket from her closet, one with a hood to prepare to brave the rain.

She ran down the stairs to her father peeking out the window, evidently assessing the slickness of the roads. "Go slowly, tonight, won't you?" he asked, concern practically written across his forehead.

"Of course," Violet said, giving her dad a quick hug for reassurance and searching for her car keys on the counter.

"It's getting dark so early now, it'll be snowing before we know it," Mr. Gray added, seeming to stall his daughter heading out into the blackened monsoon outside.

"Don't remind me," Violet spoke, smiling at him before waving a brief goodbye and heading out the door to the garage.

The garage door gaped open, allowing the harsh winds to spray a thin layer of their disorganized collection of storage boxes with water. The mess in the garage got worse every day, as if it multiplied little by little until it cluttered the entire floor of the garage with junk. The only clear space was a pathway from the door to Mr. Gray's car, and then from the car out of the building. As a result, Violet's hatchback sat slightly further down the drive, littered with speckles of water droplets.

She pulled her hood up over her blonde hair and dashed out of the garage, kicking up a splash of water behind her with every stride. She slipped her fingers in the handle and slammed the door closed, already feeling a chill climbing up her spine.

The key shifted into the ignition, bringing the engine to life and setting Violet off down the street at a slightly slower-than-usual pace.

Tanner lived on the opposite side of town, in what she and Emmy referred to as the "rich neighborhood". Yvonne also lived nearby. The houses were huge, beautifully finished, with nice yards and expensive outdoor landscaping. Tanner didn't seem like the other students who lived in the neighborhood. Typically Violet saw students who lived in this area as materialistic and really brand-sensitive. She specifically recalled a sophomore girl laughing at a knock-off The North Face jacket a freshman girl wore last year, claiming it was "The North *Fake*." Meanwhile, Tanner seemed to wear the same comfortable hoodie to school everyday.

When she parked, she rushed up to his front door and rapped on the beautifully moulded white door, noting the large, fall-themed wreath framing the peephole as she did. The door swung open in response and Tanner ushered her inside quickly, offering to rid her of her soaked jacket.

"I can throw it in the dryer if you want?" he offered politely.

"That's alright," Violet replied, not wanting to be a burden.

Tanner set the jacket hanging off the railing beside a few other soaked jackets and led her to a basement door just past it, letting her follow him down the stairs to a large space. To the right of the staircase there was a huge bedroom area with guitars and movie posters covering the walls and a huge PC setup, lit with a ton of colored LED lights. In front of her was a huge set of bookcases seemingly documenting a series of classic novels, alongside sci-fi, and along the bottom rows lay different, vintage gaming consoles with their respective controllers, also lit with LED light strips. Finally, to the left was another wide open space, hosting a living room set of a huge reclining couch, two ottomans, and two love seats which sat opposite to a notably large bathroom. A bar rested at the far wall, hiding a mini-fridge and a microwave. It was almost as if the entire basement was an apartment on its own.

"Look who's here!" Tanner called to a set of three friends set upon the furniture. On one of the loveseats sat two of the friends. Dani, a short, feminine presenting person, was sitting on the other's lap. Violet recalled Dani announcing they identified as gender non-binary the year before.

"I think you know Dani, right?" Tanner asked. Violet nodded, and Dani waved with a smile. "Well, this is Mark, their boyfriend," Tanner added.

Mark did a chin nod at Violet, keeping his arms firmly wrapped around Dani.

"And this," Tanner continued, turning to a tall, very thin boy sitting cross-legged on an ottoman, "is Neil!"

"Oh, I remember you!" Violet chirped quickly with a smile.

"You do?" Neil replied, glancing a skeptical eye in her direction.

"Yeah—We were in the same fifth grade class. We were the narrators in the class play! The Ugly Duckling, right?" Violet also remembered Neil asking her to be his girlfriend the week after that, and letting him down, but she didn't think that was the right thing to bring up.

"Oh, yeah. I didn't think you'd remember." His voice was almost somber as his eyes refocused on the television on the wall in front of them, clenching between his fists a throw pillow which looked certainly more attractive than it was comfortable.

"Alright!" Dani called, breaking the strange tension in the room. They had a remote in hand, pointing it at the television on which Netflix was cued up to a movie entitled *Rubber,* "It's movie time!"

"What's *Rubber*?" Violet asked innocently with a touch of confusion.

Dani smirked and clicked the play button. "The greatest film you'll ever see." They placed the remote beside them and leaned their head back beside Mark's.

Tanner took a seat on the sofa and patted the space beside him, inviting Violet to sit. She obliged, sitting slightly too upright. She wasn't quite comfortable enough yet to relax.

"Basically," Tanner began to explain in a whisper, "it's about a telekinetic car tire that rolls around the desert blowing shit up."

Violet cracked a wide smile. "What?" she asked in a strong tone of disbelief.

"Just consider yourself lucky you missed *The Velocipastor* last week."

"What!?" Violet echoed again.

"Shhh…" Tanner hushed her, smiling. This was obviously the reaction he'd wanted. He leaned back into the couch, making room for Violet beside him. It took a few minutes but eventually, she did rest herself beside him.

"Whoa, you're cold," he whispered, grabbing her arm to feel the goosebumps she'd had since she first stepped into the rain.

Violet offered a lighthearted chuckle. "I mean, a bit."

"Here, I'll grab a blanket." He hustled out of his seat and over to a closet, shuffled through the collection of blankets before deciding on one and returning to the still warm spot on the couch and tossed one edge of the blanket over Violet's legs.

"I grabbed the softest one, since I know you're kinda picky about blankets," he teased.

Violet grinned, pulling the blanket up over her shoulders and, daringly, scootched herself closer to Tanner so she could rest her head on his shoulder.

In response, he wrapped his arm around her, gliding his thumb along the goosebumps on her arm. Violet noticed it felt natural and comfortable, not forced. He was still wearing that same hoodie she knew him for, a deep blue, waffle knit pattern. It looked like it should have been uncomfortable, but it was surprisingly soft, likely from being worn so often. It was really quite nice.

*   *   *

By the time the movie ended, all five members of the audience were on their feet clapping. Dani was right, the film really was great (in a satirical, laugh-at-it-with-your-friends sort of way).

"I'm sorry, I thought I came here for a bad movie night, but you've just shown us a masterpiece," Violet yelled in Dani's direction.

They laughed heartily and shrugged. "It's so bad, it's good."

Mark laughed along with them, but Neil still sat cross-legged, hugging the throw-pillow tightly to his chest and avoiding eye contact.

Then, Violet recognized it was time to pack up and leave. She bid her farewells and Tanner walked her back up the stairs.

"You sure you don't want to stay?" he asked.

"I mean, I want to, but I promised my dad I'd be home before ten. I think the rain's freaking him out," Violet admitted.

"Okay, well," Tanner said, grabbing her jacket from the banister. "Let me know when you're back safe."

"You bet," Violet said, pulling on her jacket.

Once it was successfully zipped, she looked up at him. There was a silence between them, something expectant, but after a few moments with no hints taken, Violet reached around for the doorknob.

"Um, you should come again next week!" Tanner barked out hastily.

Violet looked back at him over her shoulder and answered, "Yeah, okay."

She exited the door with a smiley goodbye and returned to her car, parked neatly in the cul-de-sac just at the end of the driveway.

She slammed the car door and shifted into drive to head back. She had just enough time to make it back before ten.

A few stressful red lights and two dimly lit side streets later, Violet was pulling her car into her driveway and her hood back over her ears. The rain had slowed a little, but still not enough.

With a hand on the door, she wondered if maybe Tanner didn't kiss her for a reason. The moment felt right. She had waited for it, but he didn't take the bait. Maybe it wasn't obvious enough? As she contemplated the situation, stalling her exit from the vehicle and into the sprinkle of rain outside, she felt a vibration in her back pocket.

She slipped her phone out, the bright light burning slightly in the dark car.

TANNER

I meant to tell you, I'm picking the movie next week. Its Sharknado. :)

VIOLET

Wow. That sounds almost as good as Velocipastor.

TANNER

If you need to catch up, you can always stop by tomorrow night? I wouldn't mind watching it again with you.

Violet felt the corners of her mouth curving upward.

VIOLET

Very chivalrous. How could I refuse? :)

Then, with a sudden burst of energy, Violet pushed her way through the rain and back inside the house.

CHAPTER TWENTY-ONE

Tap tap tap, Violet's pen slapped against the table while she absentmindedly floated through the morning math class on Monday. She found her eyes drifting away from the numbers and resting on the clock and considering exactly how criminal it was to have every teenager in the area wake up at 6am so they can come and learn some advanced mathematics.

Today was "Probability Day!" as noted by the overstretched word-art style banner across the top of her teacher's slideshow.

"So you'll be making your own questions about probability and giving it to a peer to respond to. Find your partners and start writing," the teacher instructed, allowing the classroom to burst into speech almost immediately.

"I've already got mine," Xander said confidently, pulling a chair up to one side of Travis's desk as usual.

"What?" Travis replied as Violet dragged her chair to sit opposite him.

"There is a 99% chance Mr. Davis says 'dicey' in a given class period. What are the odds he says it again on Tuesday?" Xander's voice was rather pragmatic, but Travis had already begun a loud belly-laugh, attracting the attention of some nearby groups.

"Nice roast!" Travis called.

Violet laughed under her breath while she pulled a fresh piece of paper from her bag. As she slipped it out from between the bent edges of her folder, a vibration moved the bag, spiraling from its front pocket.

She reached her hand over to grab her phone and peeked at the messages she received.

TANNER

Hey, I know you said you've been working with Jess in the library during lunch, but if you want to eat in

the cafeteria for a change, we have a
spot at our table. :)

Violet considered the offer for only a few
moments. She knew she didn't want to keep sneaking
her lunch into the library and she was starting to feel
as though she was impeding Jess's ability to get work
done.

VIOLET

Sold! Meet you by the locker?

She placed her device back into its pocket and
rose from her bent position over her bag to finally
begin her work on the assignment.

"You sure look smiley," Xander noted, with
the half-assed scribbles of his question set before him,
waiting to be answered.

"Tanner just told me I could come sit at his
table at lunch instead of eating with Jess in the
Library," Violet replied softly, trying to push past the
subject.

"Jess *Daniels*? Isn't she trying to make that
gay kid's club?" Travis asked, looking up from the
work he never actually started.

Violet rolled her eyes. "It's not a gay kid's club, it's a Gay-Straight Alliance," she explained.

"Sounds like a gay kid's club," Travis blew her off.

"I'm not gay, and I'm joining," Violet spoke, her tone becoming colder and her eyes narrowing.

"Then people are going to think you're a lesbian, which, hey," he held his hands up in a defensive gesture, "I'm totally cool with." His smirk was sleazy, as if he was already fantasizing about it. Violet wanted to gag at his bigoted commentary. Fetishizing lesbians while simultaneously being homophobic was a ridiculous irony she didn't think he'd understand even if she *tried* to explain it to him.

"I don't think anyone thinks she's a lesbian," Xander offered, splicing through the tension like a hot butter knife. The comment was obviously a joke, given the widely known secret that he and Violet had sex, but he still sounded somewhat uncomfortable with the conflict.

By some miracle, the morning announcements managed to cut their conversation short.

"Good Morning, Bearcats! Welcome to another exciting day at Northridge High School!"

Their math teacher begged the class to hush and listen.

The announcements were as basic and uninteresting as ever.

1. Lunch today is gross and undercooked, as always
2. The current Book Club read is a fantasy romance (she assumed)
3. The Football team lost to their rivals, but beat a school with an equally unimpressive team.
4. The Key Club is doing that same Food Bank service activity this week as they did last week, and…

"Now for a special announcement from Principal Mick!"

The microphone made a few tapping noises during the pause, indicating the passage of the device into Principal Mick's hand.

Fake It till You Make It

"Good morning, students! This is Principal Mick with an exciting announcement. I've worked very hard the last week or so to plan a last-minute event for you students to celebrate the amazing year we've had so far. With the help of the student council, this year we'll be hosting our first Winter Formal in nearly ten years! So ladies, get your best dresses, and gentlemen, grab a suit and tie, it will certainly be an event you don't want to miss!"

Violet couldn't help but wonder for a brief moment how Dani felt about the ladies and gentlemen commentary, but that thought was quickly eclipsed by the words of Jess from the week before. She was convinced Principal Mick would do something to distract from his refusal to allow the GSA. Maybe this was it?

*   *   *

Violet sat beside Tanner at his table he held with his friends in the corner of the lunchroom. She could see the entire cafeteria from their position, and she couldn't help but notice the vacant table in the center by the large cement support where she and Yvonne used to sit. She had yet to catch where she might have gone, but she also considered that

Yvonne was avoiding her as much as she wanted to avoid Yvonne.

Chemistry was awkward enough, day to day, but at least it was an easy shift. Usually their three-man group of friends had to team off into a set of two as lab partners while whoever was left worked with the odd-man out of the *other* three-person friend group that sat two tables down. All Violet had to do was move her seat over to their table and leave as soon as the bell rang. She wasn't sure what Yvonne was doing about lunch, but it didn't matter as long as Violet had a place to be.

"Winter formal sounds so lame," Mark groaned.

"We're going," Dani said between bites of their gross and undercooked lunch. "For no other reason than that I can wear a suit and watch that discriminatory douche throw a fit about it."

"I'm going to need a more romantic proposal than that," Mark chuckled, poking Dani in the side.

"It could be kind of fun. I've never gone to homecoming or anything," Tanner admitted.

"Never?" Violet questions.

"Nope. Usually Neil and I just hang out and play video games," he said, nodding over at Neil, who still managed to avoid all forms of eye-contact with Violet.

"Awh, come on. Neil looks like he'd be a dancing machine!" Violet crowed, attempting to make a sort of connection with him.

It failed.

"I'd rather pluck my own eyes out, besides, I'll probably have to work."

Violet's shoulders sank a little, and she went back to scanning the room to see where Yvonne might have been sitting.

When the bell rang, Violet tossed the remains of her lunch in the trash and gathered her bag. While most of the table went off to the right, Dani and Violet were headed to the left.

"See you later!" Violet called to Tanner and Mark, and she guessed Neil too, though she wasn't totally certain if it mattered to him.

"Where are you headed?" Dani asked.

"Art," Violet replied.

"Really? Me too. Ceramics," they expressed with a smile.

"Painting. Though we've been spending a lot of time practicing proportions and shadows. We've only done, like, two paintings so far."

The art hallway was only just around the corner from the cafeteria. Their classroom doors were already coming up.

"Hey, so, are you and Tanner going to be a serious thing?" Dani spoke. Violet still wasn't prepared to answer that question. It had only been a few days since they had started hanging out after all.

"Oh, I'm not sure," she admitted.

"But you like him?" they pressed.

"I mean, yeah. He's a really great guy."

"Then what aren't you sure about?"

The question made Violet pause. Honestly, she wasn't sure. She felt comfortable with him, maybe more comfortable than she felt with Xander. But then again, Xander always had a sort of stiff energy. Maybe comfort wasn't the right measure. She wanted Tanner to kiss her, surely that meant something.

She felt her head beginning to spiral around at the sudden critical self-evaluation she was performing.

Was she attracted to him? Well, no. He wasn't particularly attractive to her. She was really attracted to his personality, but that seemed more like a sign of friendship than a relationship. So why did she want him to kiss her?

Maybe because that's what teenage girls were supposed to do. They're supposed to make-out in the dark during a movie. They're supposed to want boys to kiss them. It's a staple to kiss at the end of the night. Was she even that disappointed when he didn't kiss her?

She suddenly wasn't sure.

"I don't know," she finally said, "I just think it's a little new and I still want to get to know him a bit." It was certain that it was a lie, but it sounded like a good one leaving her lips.

"I guess that's fair," Dani nodded, understanding, "But I know he's definitely into you. And we all like you too. Just so you know," they clarified with a shrug.

They had stopped just before Dani's open ceramics classroom door.

"Well, see ya!" they called, preparing to enter the classroom, but one more subject tugged at Violet's brain, ringing in her ears.

"Wait, um, I have a question," she stopped Dani from going any further. They turned with a quizzical look and waited for Violet's question. "Neil. He doesn't seem to like me." There was a pause. "Actually, he seems to hate me," she confessed with a sheepish grin in an attempt to be lighthearted, though she knew deep down it actually bothered her.

"Oh," Dani laughed, "Yeah, well. He's been Tanner's friend for a *loooong* time. Mark and I just think he's super clingy and possessive for whatever reason. He'll come around to you," they waved her question off as a non-concern.

"Is that what happened with you?" Violet questioned.

"No, not really, but we weren't exactly interested in starting a personal relationship with Tanner, either," they explained. "I think he's just worried about Tanner spending more time with you and less time with him, you know, assuming you two get together. It's always hard to integrate new relationships into old ones. For the first few months, I swear, all couples do is hang out with each other and ditch their friends."

Her words stung a little. They made Violet think of Yvonne and how little she and Emmy got to see her on the weekends when she and Steven became official. She felt the heat of resentment forming inside of her as she considered her current situation. It could have been possible that Steven was a big part of the reason she and Yvonne were so out of sync now, and if that was the case, what would happen if she started dating Tanner?

CHAPTER TWENTY-TWO

Violet flipped through the collection of notes from Tanner in her bag, pulling out the most recent one. They'd turned it into something of an ice breaker where each letter contained some new information about their locker-mate.

V,

I've had the Shins stuck in my head all day.

I don't know if you listen to them at all, but if you don't, you should listen to "Simple Song". I think you'd like it.

One the topic of things you'd like, my mom's getting snacks for movie night.

Any recommendations? I'm thinking popcorn and raisinets..

I know, I'm a grandmother. Don't laugh too hard.

−T.

Violet found herself flipping back and forth between her classwork and writing her response note in English. She considered how easy it would be to just send him a text with her favorite candies, but then it took away the excitement and mystery of finding a new note in the locker. She loved the little surprises, and she figured he must too. Otherwise, he might have stopped writing long ago.

T,

I'll add Simple Song to my list. I've been listening to "Kaleidoscope" by Great Big World on repeat while getting ready the last few mornings. Pretty sure my dad is sick of listening to it.

Also, I won't laugh, but you have to promise to be chill when I say I actually kind of... don't like chocolate? I KNoW. UNameRicaN, oR whateveR. I'm more of a fRuity caNdy peRsoN, like Skittles oR Swedish Fish. See you at luNch!

xo V

The days had started to move more smoothly. Emmy had stopped trying to intervene in the drama between Violet and Yvonne, resigning to believe that the issue would resolve itself soon. The conversation around Violet and Xander had all but died out, and with the news of Winter Formal coming up, students were suddenly way more focused on finding their dates than anything else, though Jess was still insanely certain it was all a distraction tactic.

As an important part of the student council, she knew she couldn't simply boycott the event, but that also meant she'd have to work overtime to solve the GSA issue. As a result, Violet was offering her services to Jess on an as-needed basis.

Of course, she was *always* needed, so it felt more like a part-time job.

As Violet packed her things up at the end of the day, Ms. Elliot, her chemistry teacher, approached with a manila folder between her fingers.

"Violet, Jess Daniels said you'll be seeing her this afternoon. Is that correct?" she inquired.

"Yeah," Violet replied with a hint of confusion.

"She asked me to print these. It's the district information on use of school spaces for non-school sponsored events and organizations, and a few copies of the necessary forms." Ms. Elliot had a very warm smile as she spoke, handing the folder over to Violet. "It turns out we *can* host GSA meetings after school, it just won't be an official school club. That also means we won't be able to advertise it within school walls."

Suddenly, the tasks Jess had Violet completing made way more sense. She had been checking around for student groups on Facebook and making flashy fliers for meetings in various sizes, probably for a massive social media campaign she'd have to launch just so students would know about the club if they weren't allowed to use the school announcements, news, or walls, even.

Violet opened the folder and rifled through as if to be sure everything was there, though she wasn't certain exactly what she was looking for.

"Got it. I'll let her know. Thank you!"

Ms. Elliot moved through the clog of students at her doorway to prepare for her hall duty, and Violet turned back to finish her packing. The ball rang and the students crowding around the door melted into the masses in the hallway, leaving a mostly quiet room, which made it extra obvious when Yvonne walked past her without so much as a glance or a goodbye, again.

Emmy appeared to follow but stopped at Violet before reaching the door. "Hey," she called, forcing Violet to turn and acknowledge the friend she'd scarcely spoken to in the last week, "Are we good?" she asked. Her usually vibrant tone was somehow meek and anxious.

Violet nodded before she spoke. "Yeah, I think so," she said punctuating it with a pause before adding, "*You* didn't tell me I was blowing any guy who looked at me."

"I don't think she said that," Emmy obviously felt the pain that escaped Violet's lips impulsively. Her brown eyes were invisible as a result of the bright fluorescent lights leaving a glare right where they'd be through her glasses. Violet couldn't quite get a read on why she'd say those words—if it was a feeble attempt to abate the issue or if she was trying to dismiss the fact that it was said.

Truthfully, Violet didn't remember exactly what Yvonne said; it was possible those weren't the exact words. All she remembered for sure was the aggressive feeling of being stabbed in the gut over and over with a rusty spoon.

"I really wish you'd back me up here," Violet confessed.

"I want to, V, it's just," Emmy's nose pinched up as if she'd smelled something rotten, "I get where both of you are coming from."

"What!?" Violet felt a jab in her gut again.

"Look, I don't agree with what she said about you being a slut! That'd just be hypocritical," she added the last comment as a joke. Violet did not laugh. Emmy continued, "But I do think something's changed. You used to tell us everything, now it seems like you're specifically keeping things from us, and we just can't figure out why. It feels a lot like you're… I don't know… pulling away?"

Violet knew her face must have been so red, but she couldn't formulate a response. Instead of a repeated stab, this one was more like a slow twist of a rusty spoon in her gut.

Guilt.

Emmy was right, but Violet still couldn't figure out why she couldn't just tell her everything that's been on her mind. The guilt shifted to embarrassment. The phrases were itching to spill out of her mouth like a river breaking through a dam, but every time they were on the verge of materializing, they retreated back into her brain. It all happened so quickly, even Violet couldn't confront them.

The aggressive buzz of her phone on the desk stopped the stand-off. Violet broke the eye contact with Emmy to peek at the message on her phone.

TANNER

Hey, I hate to ask but its a bit of an emergency. Neil has to get to work but his ride canceled and my brother and I need to go get my dad from the airport. Is there anyway you can take him? We're at the front of the school

Escape, Violet thought.

"Tanner's friend needs a ride to work. I need to take him," she said to Emmy, still waiting for a response.

"Oh," she said. Her shoulders slumped very slightly, but Violet knew her well enough to notice. "So, are you and Tanner a thing?"

"I don't know yet," she admitted quickly, throwing her bag over her shoulder, "I'll let you know when I do," and she pushed past Emmy to meet the boys at the main entrance.

She noticed them sitting on a bench and picked up her pace slightly to get there quicker. "Hey!" she called, "You need a ride? I'm happy to help," Violet cooed a little too cheerfully at Neil.

"Yup." A classic, curt response.

"Thanks, Vi! You're the best," Tanner beamed. It was like night and day with them.

"Where do you work?" Violet asked, again trying to engage Neil in conversation.

"Jump Around," he answered.

Violet couldn't help but crack a smile. "That kid's trampoline park?" she asked, trying not to appear as though she'd laugh.

He didn't even respond. Tanner interrupted with a quick, "There's my brother! I have to go. I'll talk to you guys soon." And he scurried out of the vestibule, leaving Violet and Neil alone.

*   *   *

"I thought the petition was supposed to solve this problem?" Violet asked, skimming the series of printouts Ms. Elliot had given her earlier, spread out side by side on Jess's desk, lit by a gaudy seashell lamp.

Jess's bedroom looked as though it hadn't been updated since she was twelve. Her bedding and decorations were all beach themes, culminating in blues and tans everywhere, and punctuated by the fact that her closet doors were missing and replaced with a set of hanging beads. Violet remembered how fun she found them when Jess first put them up, but now she found them somewhat unsightly.

"All the petition means is that Principal Mick and the administrators have to reconsider. It doesn't mean we automatically get what we want," Jess replied, sitting cross-legged at the foot of her bed and clicking through various fonts on her laptop.

"Really? Then why bother? I mean, if we have a backup plan, why did we need the petition?" Violet questioned.

"It would just be a whole lot easier if we could use the school's resources to make the students aware of the group. It normalizes it in a sense, you know? Though I seriously doubt he'll listen to reason about this. He obviously hates me," Jess groaned.

Violet scoffed in response. "Whatever you think *hate* is, it has literally nothing on Neil. I don't think I even knew what it meant to be hated before today."

"What do you mean?" Jess asked.

"I drove him to work today because Tanner asked me to, and he was just dead silent for most of it. He looked at me *twice* and both times felt like he was trying to telekinetically blow my head off like that car tire in that movie we watched last weekend. I told him I hoped he had a good day and I *swear* I heard him tell me to fuck off under his breath before slamming the car door so hard I felt myself shake!"

Jess listened patiently with a grimace across her face.

"Seriously, I'm already iffy on the whole Tanner thing, and this might be a deal breaker. I don't think I can deal with that all the time," Violet finished with an exasperated sigh.

"Do you want my advice?" Jess asked. Violet appreciated the gesture but felt another pang of guilt knowing Jess only asked as a caution to avoid any retaliation like she experienced the last time she tried to be honest with her.

"Yes," Violet replied.

"I really think you should go for it with Tanner. Neil will have to get over it, and really, I think it'll be good for you," Jess said, closing the lip of her laptop to focus on her friend.

"What do you mean?" Violet pressed.

"I *mean* you spent a lot of time last week pissed at Yvonne, right? She called you a slut and you hated that. Plus Tanner is really nice to you. You like his friends, and hanging out with all of them… for the most part," she added, referring to Neil.

"What does any of that have to do with Yvonne?" Violet winced slightly when Jess mentioned her name.

Jess shrugged, running her fingers through the ends of one of her braids with pops of orange weaving throughout it. "Sluts are non-committal. They don't have boyfriends. I mean, that's the stereotype anyway, I don't appreciate the whole slut-shaming thing in the first place. But if you're really concerned about the way people see you, and if Tanner is a good guy who is treating you well, why not at least give it a shot, right?"

Violet found her head bobbing up and down in agreement. It made sense to her; strategically speaking, it was a good move. The fact that she wasn't attracted to him now didn't seem like an issue. Love at first sight was a silly cliche. She always thought that. The attraction would surely come with a little time and patience, and the idea of taking things slowly sounded strangely appealing to her at this point.

It was settled then. Whenever Tanner made the move, she would go for it.

CHAPTER TWENTY-THREE

It felt like a blink. A swift and simple *snap* separated Violet from sitting on Jess's floor to the creaky sound of warped, aged hinges stretching wide to reveal a new note resting on Tanner's set of untouched books on the top shelf of their shared locker.

Violet immediately felt drained from the soreness of the constant roller coaster movements and contractions her stomach made within the past twenty-four hours. From dealing with the anxiety of her old friends, the sheer, unadulterated hatred from Neil, a see-saw of positive and negative news coming from Jess about the GSA, and the general confusion about her relationship with Tanner, it felt like nothing short of God's interference that she didn't have abs at this point.

Regardless of how quickly the moment came, time slowed to an almost grinding halt as she stared at the letter. It seemed rather unassuming, normal even, resting on its legs, standing in a gable shape with the sharp angle of her first initial staring straight back. She imagined, for a sweet fleeting moment, the letter crawling away, inching like a worm to hide behind the books so she could deal with it some other time, but it didn't. No matter how innocent it appeared, her gut was screaming up through the chasm of her rib cage. This was show time.

Violet exhaled slowly and snatched at the paper quickly as though she were ripping off a band-aid and unfolded it so quickly a passerby might think the edges were burning her skin. It didn't need to, though, her whole body already felt like fire.

Two words, a single line, scribbled in all caps in the middle of the paper. No address, no signature. They weren't needed.

WINTER FORMAL?

She knew her answer already. She'd decided on it the night before. So that's what it would be.

Violet reached for her phone but stopped. She wondered if Tanner might be feeling the same way she was. His stomach might be twisted in knots or performing flips that would make Olympic gymnasts jealous, just like her. It was oddly satisfying to think he might be sharing that feeling with her. The thought was somewhat cruel, but it was also soothing to know they might be experiencing this together, and for that reason she chose to leave her response in the locker as well.

YES.

She mimicked his same, single line, all caps message with hers, pointedly choosing not to punctuate with an exclamation point. No one wants to seem too eager.

The locker door snapped back into its naturally locked position, and Violet sped off to her next class with the heels on her boots clicking along the floor, leaving the future stored between those metal walls for just a few more classes.

*   *   *

"This is so great. We never have a group to go with so Dani's mom and step-dad always take us out to it and it's always mad awkward," Mark said. His arm was hidden under the table, but it was bent in such a way that suggested it was resting on Dani's knee beside him. Violet couldn't help but notice Tanner was sitting slightly closer to her today, close enough to put his hand on her knee.

"Yes, we should all go somewhere nice, like a hibachi place or a steakhouse," Tanner commented.

"Are you paying?" Dani scoffed. "Let's just pull up to Taco Bell. Nothing warms the heart like a tostada," they smirked, biting into an almost comically horrible version of a taco that had been served for lunch that day.

Neil didn't grab a lunch tray that day. Instead, he sat staring at the scratched up laminate covering the table, his eyes glazing over. Violet considered that might be the only thing worse than watching paint dry.

"Neil, I know it's not your thing, but you should really come," Tanner spoke, breaking Violet's train of thought.

"Not a chance. I'll just hang back and play video games like always," he grumbled.

The table grew more uncomfortable. Violet looked to Tanner who was already looking at Dani who was picking a stringy tomato out of their school taco.

"Well, offer stands if you change your mind," Mark said, breaking the discomfort, though not dissolving it completely.

"Oh, and by the way, if you want to come by a little early tonight, I could use some help setting up the snacks before movie night?" Tanner asked Violet, obviously trying to change the subject.

She glanced over at Dani, who was again using their strange series of questionable foods wrapped within a soggy flour tortilla to occupy them in the series of apparent social crises at their lunch table.

"Sure," Violet smiled, hopefully quick enough to not appear hesitant. She'd already begun to overthink it.

*   *   *

Bowls lined a card table popped up against the side wall of Tanner's basement in a gradient set of blue colors, clearly dragged down from his mother's kitchen cabinets. The back row of the darkest blues held the remains of the bowl of off-brand white cheddar popcorn (Dani was convinced it was the best), followed by Cool Ranch Doritos crumbs for Mark, and a bag of kettle cooked potato chips for Neil which served only as a vessel for the French onion dip nearly scraped clean beside them. In a slightly smaller bowl, the most medium toned of all the blues, was a bowl of buttery, yet unpopped, microwave popcorn kernels which Tanner had gingerly sprinkled an entire box of Raisinets into, thus leaving a series of questionable melted smears along the edges of the bowl. At the front of the table, the two smallest bowls, practically white, was the ghost of a sharing size bag of skittles (which Tanner insisted to Violet she did not have to actually share), and a standard sized box of Swedish fish which remained untouched in the bowl. Most notably however, was the large mylar balloon of a shark, floating in the corner of the room.

"What is that!?" Violet had immediately burst into laughter upon entering the basement.

"I told mom what movie we were watching, she said she saw it at the supermarket and couldn't help picking it up. Said it was too cute." Tanner smiled and shrugged.

"Too cute? I'm not sure she really gets the essence of *Sharknado*," Violet giggled, falling back onto the couch.

The shark was now the unfortunate third-wheel to Tanner and Violet, who sat, shoulder to shoulder on the couch after Dani and Mark absolutely insisted Neil come home in their car, strategically leaving the two alone with the shark to ensure they didn't get into too much trouble.

This wasn't the first time these two had sat alone on this couch, but there was something different about the energy now. Tanner stayed facing the television, while Violet was angled sideways, stretching across the length of the couch with her legs draped playfully over Tanner's lap.

"So, Winter Formal," Tanner said, breaking the silence.

Violet nodded. "Yup." She forced an awkward grin, unsure of what would come next.

"That's like, a date, right?"

Another pause. A slower nod.

"Yeah…" One eyebrow lifted on Violet's forehead, anticipating an elaboration.

"So you might say that *we're* dating."

Violet held back a cringe, imagining this is exactly how she sounded that last time she was alone with a boy on his couch with no parents around.

"Yeah, I might say that," she offered in a half-tease, half reassuring tone.

"And people who date sometimes, kiss," he said, waiting a moment, "Right?"

The line was so wonderfully awful, it took so much of Violet's self-control to not laugh at the sheer discomfort of it all. Up to this point, things fit together with them. They felt natural. She wondered if even Tanner thought this was the right next step for them or if his hormones were just making him impulsive. Surely he hadn't thought this conversation out in his head beforehand. Whereas Violet played this scenario in her head over and over with different lines and motions. This was not one of her anticipated outcomes.

Steer into the skid. Xander's voice echoed in her head again. She really shouldn't be thinking of Xander at this moment, but still, she nodded and lowered her voice to a whisper. "Right," she said in her best attempt at a sultry-tone. It would have been better had it not been punctuated with a clearing of her throat, followed by an apologetic repeat. "Right," she said, a bit louder.

Tanner leaned into her and pressed his lips against hers quickly, peeling them off like he'd done something wrong.

Violet let the feeling of his mouth on hers linger for a moment, assessing it as one might consider the subtler notes of a perfume, trying to pick out something familiar. His lips were rough, probably from all the anxious chewing of his bottom lip she'd noticed during the movie. It was so quick, but still she noticed, and even though she noticed, she certainly wouldn't tell him. Instead, she leaned her head closer, inviting him to kiss her again.

The second kiss went on longer, resting lightly again whenViolet's fingers wrapped around the back of his neck, pulling him closer to her.

The energy shifted almost immediately.

Tanner slipped himself out from the confines of Violet's legs and rested beside her hip, pushing her backward so her neck laid against the arm of the couch. Her hand stayed firmly beside his ear, her eyes closed as she shifted his position to kiss her more deeply. His mouth opened, naturally indicating Violet to do the same. His tongue dove to the back of her throat, dancing between her cheeks in a way that reminded Violet of her drunk uncle at her second cousin's wedding.

What a mood killer.

She lightly pulled her head back as if she were coming up for air, and in a last-moment effort to not appear too much like she was pushing him away, she lightly bit down on his lower lip while he dragged it away from her mouth, expelling deep, heavy breaths.

When she'd read about that little move in *Cosmo* she wondered how it wouldn't hurt, though she also secretly hoped it hurt at least enough to keep his tongue in his own mouth for a while. She smacked her lips together to stop the instinct she felt to wipe his spit off from around her mouth. It was still a little too wet, but it was at least manageable.

"Wow, um," Tanner paused, still hovering over her like a starving vampire. "I'm sorry, I don't really do this kind of stuff much."

"Much?" Violet echoed.

Tanner exhaled an embarrassed laugh. "Never," he corrected.

Yet another scenario Violet had not considered. Somehow, in the last few weeks, she had become *experienced*. At least more experienced than Tanner was.

"Are you…" Violet started to ask before she really considered it. She instantly regretted that decision. She'd already exercised so much control that night, she was bound to slip up eventually. "You know," she smiled, giving the question a more casual tone, "A virgin?"

Tanner sat up a bit straighter, allowing Violet to prop herself up on her elbows as she waited for the answer. "Yeah," he responded honestly. "Is that a problem?" he asked, more as though he was genuinely concerned rather than defensive.

"No, of course not. I mean," she continued, "I haven't done all too much myself."

"Really?" Tanner replied. Violet didn't take the time to consider the implications of that question.

"Yeah. Well," she paused for a second before finishing the thought. "I'm not a virgin, but I don't think it's a big deal… Virginity, I mean!" she clarified.

"Right, so," Tanner exhaled and looked around slightly for the right words to formulate his next move. "Do you want to—"

"No!" Violet called instinctively. In the millisecond, she swore it looked like she'd punched Tanner in the chest. He leaned back quickly to give her space. She kept the distance between them short as she quickly got up on her knees and looked him directly in the eye. "No, just, no yet, I mean! I don't think we should rush this."

The relief in Tanner's eyes was almost palpable. He must have thought she meant she didn't want to have sex with him specifically. At that time, he may have been right. Violet didn't feel particularly called to have sex right then. He deserved to have his first time be with someone he really cared about and who really cared about him.

"I just don't want you to regret it," she explained, attempting to separate out the complex collage of thoughts swirling in her mind into functional sentences.

Tanner's cheeks filled with a smile. He relaxed his shoulders and closed the gap between them once more, placing a light kiss on her lips. "I don't think I'll regret it," his words came soft and slow. He outdid her in the sultriness for sure.

"Let's wait," she croaked out again, in a subtle panic, "for something special."

Tanner backed up and nodded, considering her suggestion. "Winter Formal?" The eagerness in his voice was not particularly well disguised.

Violet smiled to cover herself as she imagined that scenario: a romantic evening of dancing, getting all dressed up, cuddling up under the blankets at home, and drinking cocoa to warm up. The extraneous thoughts drained out of her ears, slithering away from her body. Her body released the pent up tension. The night seemed like a textbook special event. Almost every teen drama featured a spicy sex-scene after the prom. The mood would be set in a way that greatly rivaled any of her previous sexual experiences, and that's exactly what she was hoping for.

Mimicking the note she'd written only just that morning, she replied simply and positively, "Yes."

CHAPTER TWENTY-FOUR

A quiet settled in Violet's room. The tip of her nose was brightly lit by the computer screen as she scrolled through pages of advice on the *Cosmopolitan* website, desperate for something to help her prepare for the night of Winter Formal, now a little over a week away.

The articles had gotten so repetitive, it seemed. The pro-tips all seemed the same and nothing seemed like the easy type of beginner move she wanted. She supposed that's why they were called pro-tips, not beginner tips. She was teetering the line between wanting to have a good experience and not seeming like she was a professional sex worker.

She found herself tapping the arrow keys and making her way down the page way quicker than she had in the past. Every suggestion or tip started to read like a question that her brain immediately refuted.

Ball stimulation? *Yup. Seen it.*

Sex toys? *Definitely not going to happen.*

Grinding? *Mhm.*

Outercourse? *Understood.*

Sexting? *Got it.*

A sex playlist? *Okay, that's new, but still, no thanks.*

She had officially given up on checking the porn sites. She learned quickly that all porn did was make her feel more inadequate.

Her tapping finally fell out of rhythm as she came across a simple Q&A which caught her attention.

"How do I know if I've had an orgasm?"

She skimmed casually, as if *Cosmo* would know she was overly eager to see the response, but her eyes narrowed when she reached a short, single line response.

"If you have to ask, you haven't."

Violet groaned and rolled her eyes. She was convinced she had. The physical responses all lined up with the expectations, but the major difference in the way she recalled the experience and the way the interviewees on *Cosmo* did was simple: it wasn't this insane life-changing experience for her. She didn't keep wanting to go back for more or do it again. It just *didn't matter*.

As her tapping grew more pointed and aggressive, she was interrupted by a harsh vibration on her desk. She snatched her device and swiped open the messages to read.

EMMY
Hey, I know we haven't hung out in a while but I still need a dress for formal and I'll die if I have to go with my mom...

Violet turned her head to see the beautiful formal dress she'd already gotten. She'd gotten a floor length gown, a-line, with a slit going up the left side. It was nearly impossible to find a dress that didn't have a little leg showing, that just seemed to be the style. She loved keeping it just outside of the closet so it would catch the light from the window. The dress was a simple black stretchy fabric with a double layer of glittering tulle over top, reminding her of a nighttime sky with all the stars. She never really imagined herself as the type to wear an all-black dress to a dance, but this one was pretty enough to justify it.

It seemed that somehow all this time she'd spent out of the house now only prompted Mr. Gray to want to spoil her which he seemed to believe was their bonding time. He offered to buy a dress for her when she told him she'd be attending the event. They'd gone to the local mall only a few days after Tanner had asked Violet to go. Violet picked out three styles she liked, tried them on and made her decision in the matter of an hour. It felt good to have some part of the evening planned already and go so smoothly.

Regardless of the fact that her dress had already been picked, she felt obliged to join Emmy. She was never really too upset with her after all, the only issue making her pause was the uncomfortable conversation that might come from the two of them being alone again.

Her eyes swapped between the screen of her phone and her laptop, still open on the desk in front of her. These were her choices. Dress shopping with Emmy or continue to read about what sex positions she and Tanner should use based on their Zodiac signs. The winner was obvious.

VIOLET

Yeah, let's go. I'll pick you up in 10.

She grabbed her keys and rushed out the door, remembering to exit out of the browser windows first. One step outside forced her to turn right back around and grab a thicker jacket. The winds lashed against her face, leaving red in its place. She hopped in the car, already cleared of the annoyingly thin layer of frost by her father that morning, and got on the road.

Emmy, as always, was quick to escape her mother's house, hopping into Violet's passenger side seat and beginning to chat, almost as if nothing had changed between them.

"Okay!" she called, slamming the door quickly to stop the frosty breezes from infiltrating the now toasty vehicle. "I have a couple of dresses I found online that I think would look good. One of them is short but super pretty. Do you think it'd be weird to wear a short dress? I know everyone's going for the long ones," her sentences ran together as

273

always in a mixture of excitement and probably anxiety.

"I think a few people are going short. It'll definitely stand out," Violet replied, unable to stop herself from falling back into their old patterns of speech almost immediately. It felt good to have this familiar banter and pretend like their last conversation never happened.

"Are you going with anyone?" Violet inquired as they rolled down the side streets.

"No. It's going to be a girl's night for us," Emmy said, the words loaded with intention. She was trying specifically to not bring up Yvonne. She pulled her slightly fogged glasses off her nose and attempted to wipe them clean.

Violet's curiosity got in the way of that plan quickly. "Yvonne's not bringing Steven?" she asked, pointedly.

"Um, no," Emmy replied, "I don't think they're going to last much longer," she confessed.

Violet glanced over at Emmy briefly before returning her eyes to the road. "Is she okay?" she asked, her affection for her friend betraying her resolve to avoid the topic altogether.

"Well," Violet could tell Emmy was debating on telling her what had gone on since she and Yvonne weren't exactly friends at the moment, but as always, it seemed as though the secrets between the three of them always came to light. "He called her a slut," she said.

Violet's jaw dropped. The triumphant, karmic irony of the moment was not lost on her, but still, she was more confused than anything. Emmy could tell.

"He's kind of a dick," Emmy finalized her thoughts.

"How, though?" Violet pressed, still bewildered, trying to make sense of it in her head. "I mean, we both thought they were going to do it, and wasn't she the one who put a stop to it? How does that make her a slut?"

Emmy grimaced. "I think his exact words were that she's a 'tease, just like your slutty friends.' End quote."

Violet's jaw dropped wider with her eyes opening to a similar size. "And she didn't dump him immediately!?"

"No, she just hung up on him and broke down," she said, pausing before deciding to add, "she was actually supposed to come with me to the mall today."

It was then, in that quiet between them that Violet decided to change the subject. She hated to admit it, but she seemed to have grown a bit of a soft spot for Yvonne, even after what she'd said.

*   *   *

When Winter Formal came, Mark picked Violet up in his car last, allowing her to climb in the back seat with Tanner while Dani took up the passenger seat. Tanner matched Violet's dress with a black-on-black ensemble, broken up only with a red bowtie as Violet broke hers up with a pair of red shoes and a bold red lipstick. They offset Dani and Mark perfectly in a white and blue color scheme. Mark sported an all-white suit, which made Violet wince a little with how bright it was. It complemented Dani's bright blue suit perfectly. Their outfits were identical, just inverted, and topped off with a nice set of skinny ties in a distinctive, floral, watercolor pattern.

"It never feels normal to come to the school this late at night," Mark commented as they wandered into the south entrance of the school.

"What's not normal is hosting something called a "formal" in the same place a student tripped and fell on their ass playing field hockey the day before," Dani snorted.

"Is that a personal grievance, Dani?" Violet teased.

"This isn't just about me," they commented. "It's about all the other brave soldiers who tripped and fell on their asses before me, and anyone who will trip and fall on their ass afterward."

The gym was dark, and several teachers and administrators lined the edges, keeping their eyes out for inappropriate dance moves and some prank they likely weren't prepared for. Garlands of glittery paper snowflakes that easily could have been made by preschoolers or a rushed student council (it was unclear which) lined the folded bleachers, reflecting the lights from the DJ's setup like tiny disco balls all over. Violet felt like she was reflecting a lot of the light herself as she navigated her way through the masses, surely leaving a small trail of black glitter flecks in her wake.

For a few hours, it really felt like the stress had been let go. She waved to Emmy in a short red body-con dress, who of course came running to ask for a picture. She snapped a quick selfie with her phone before running back off to Yvonne who stood patiently waiting slightly out of view, radiating a depressing energy in a floral halter neck gown that appeared to have been hemmed just slightly too short.

Violet could only remember two slow dances, always cut short by the DJ bringing in a much more upbeat song after more than half of the crowd dissolved for lack of a date. There was one guy in a batman mask who went around offering the sadder looking girls a dance. That was definitely a clever move, especially when he was unmasked by an administrator and found to be a freshman boy trying to shoot his shot.

As the dance came to a close, couples and groups shuffled their way outside the doors again with their heels in their hands and their ties in their back pockets. The parking lot grew emptier slowly. Only a few cars remained with Violet and Tanner slipping into Mark's backseat. Mark and Dani hadn't been spotted in the dance for the last thirty minutes or so, and this fact coupled with the suspicious steaminess of the car led Violet to the pretty obvious conclusion. She only hoped they'd kept their fun to the front seat.

"Just drop us off at my place," Tanner told Mark, who nodded knowingly.

Violet spent weeks planning this out in her head. The dance ended at nine thirty so everyone would be out of the school by ten. This gave Violet about two hours before she had to head home for her curfew. At the end of the night, Tanner would borrow his dad's car to drive her home.

In his basement, he intentionally dimmed the lights as they walked down the stairs. On the card table lining the side wall sat a slim vase with a single red rose, with a little handwritten note like the ones they left for each other in their locker.

Violet smiled. "What's this?" she asked.

"A little added romance? I don't know. It felt right," he tried to justify his moves.

Violet pinched the note between two fingers and opened it as Tanner watched.

For the most beautiful girl at the Winter Formal. ♡

She read the words again and again, tracing the symbols with her eyes. The night had been so wonderful, maybe even perfect. Tanner made his move, snaking his arms around her waist from behind and resting his head on her shoulder, turning it slightly to kiss her hair, down to her cheek, her ear, and even lower to her neck.

She naturally angled her head to give him space to speckle her skin with the cool echoes of his lips against her skin. She twisted in his arms, wrapping her own around his neck and resting her lips to his. She recognized how much easier this felt now than it had the first time. He was easy to be with, romantic, sweet. It felt right to do this again with him. She just knew it would be different.

It was time; so they did.

CHAPTER TWENTY-FIVE

Tanner laid along his couch, Violet laid beside him with his chest under her ear, her arms slung over his body in a loose embrace. Tanner dragged his palms along Violet's arm, creeping lower and lower until a stray finger wiggled its way into the waistband of her pants.

A jolt of energy shot up Violet's spine as she angled herself away slightly so his hands were just out of reach.

"What's wrong?" he inquired, laying still, moving only to breathe.

"I'm just," Violet avoided eye contact as she finished the phrase, "not really in the mood."

Tanner made a disappointed face and nodded, turning his neck back to their new binge-watching material on the television screen, allowing Violet the feeling of enough comfort to return to her original space on his chest.

It had been nearly two months since the evening of Winter Formal had come and gone, and Violet was starting to really enjoy the idea of having a boyfriend. In the time since their first rendezvous, it was becoming clear that Violet could excuse herself from their X-rated activities for any reason under the sun, and she still had all the benefits of an intimate relationship. Tanner would still hold her and stroke her hair and lightly kiss her goodbye, and at the very least still see her regularly, even if they weren't having sex. It felt surprisingly nice to have a solid relationship built outside of their copulation schedule.

Unfortunately, even for Violet, she recognized that while she was very happy with a sexless relationship and keeping their more sensual evenings few and far between, Tanner didn't seem to share this sentiment.

Violet knew every time she sat alone with Tanner in his basement, it was a countdown to see what move he would make—not if he'd make a move, but which one it would be when it inevitably came. Every time she shot him down, she felt as though she was stoking an invisible fire within him which would eventually grow too large to contain.

On the night of Winter Formal, only moments after their first time together and Tanner's first time ever, he asked Violet a question she realized she was very used to lying about.

"So," he chuckled awkwardly, "was I any good?"

"Of course!" Violet replied quickly. Even if she thought otherwise, it's not like she could tell him. It would destroy him. "I was very impressed," she added. This was somewhat true. In the back of her mind, she couldn't help comparing her latest experience with her first experience with Xander. Maybe it was because neither of them really knew what they were doing, but at least Tanner… well… moved. Compared to that, she definitely was impressed, solely by the fact that he seemed to have some confidence for his first time.

That comment was evidently a significant ego-boost for him.

Meanwhile, Violet found herself cuddled up next to her new boyfriend, staring at the guitars on the wall in front of her and wondering if this time was different, or even better.

Unfortunately for her, the answer seemed to be a resounding no.

She was running out of reasons and rationalizations. It didn't seem like this was a lack of experience. It wasn't about pain; it didn't hurt. It wasn't about being with someone she really cared about, or different positions, or a lack of understanding. Sex didn't seem all it was cracked up to be.

This strange act of intimacy had the power to break up relationships, hold whole sections in popular magazine, spawn a whole genre of books, television, advertisements, and films to satisfy the world hungry for sex, but for some reason, for Violet, it was wholly undesirable. It did not seem to matter to her the way it mattered to everyone else and that made her very nervous.

And at that moment, Violet repositioned herself beside Tanner, keeping her pelvic bone a few inches away from his body, she considered finally saying it.

I don't really like having sex.

No. Those words were wrong; it was more complicated than that. It's not like she was repulsed by the idea of ever doing it again, she just didn't care if she did. It just wasn't important. If they never had sex again, that would be fine. If they did, that would also be fine, just maybe not as frequently. She felt her lips tense as she considered how to word it.

I don't care about having sex, it's just not that fun to me? Her thoughts started to question themselves.

She tipped her chin up slightly to look at Tanner's face, angled down at her from leaning against the arm of the couch, illuminated by the blue light of the television screen.

He noticed her movement, looked down and smiled softly at her, still harboring a faint glisten of disappointment in the back of his mind at having been shot down again.

Violet smiled back as sweetly as she could muster before placing a gentle peck on his lips and resettling. She couldn't tell him that. It wouldn't go over well. She wondered just barely if it might even be enough to break up, and surely it wouldn't be as amicable as her break-up with Xander had been.

No, she wouldn't say anything. She'd just keep faking it. Valentine's day was coming up, a nice, special occasion. She'd just concede to him then.

*   *   *

"Alright, class, today we're starting a creative project! You will all separate out into groups of three or four, then come and select a topic from the bucket!" Ms. Elliot shook a shallow white plastic bucket which previously held the dry-erase markers on her desk. It was now filled with small slips of folded paper. "Once that's all settled, I'll explain the requirements. Go!" she called.

Violet looked back to the group of three friends she'd infiltrated earlier this year, she made four. No problem.

"Which one of us wants to go grab a topic?" Violet asked just before feeling a tap on her shoulder.

"Hey, Vi. It's just me and Yvonne in a group of two. Any chance you'll be our third?" Emmy asked sweetly, putting on a large set of puppy-dog eyes and her most deeply placating smile.

Violet looked over at Yvonne who, surprisingly, was looking in her direction as well and offering a small, anxious smile.

"No problems here," one of Violet's almost group mates said, and with a shrug Violet got to her feet to move back to her old lab table.

"Yeah, I suppose that's fine. I'll get the topic."

Emmy looked as though she were about to burst with happiness and Violet followed her back to their seats. Emmy and Yvonne now sat with their backs to the window, on the opposite side of the table looking at Violet as she snagged a folded sheet from the bucket at the front of the room and returned to her old seat.

Yvonne reached for the paper, which Violet had set in the middle of their table, and unfurled it to reveal their topic. "Acids and Bases," she announced, flipping the words around to show her lab partners.

"Cool!" Emmy called, just slightly too cheerfully.

A brief silence fell, made less uncomfortable by the roar of student chatter around them.

"So," Yvonne spoke first. "How've you been?"

Violet was cautious going forward. "Good," she answered curtly. "Tanner's planning a romantic

Valentine's dinner for us this weekend, so I'm pretty excited about that." She wanted to bring up Tanner's name intentionally. She wanted Yvonne to know that her relationship, which Yvonne had seemed to resent so much, was going swimmingly.

"Oh, good," Yvonne nodded, dropping her eyes to the table, obviously not wanting to speak more. She looked defeated, and that made Violet feel powerful, but also slightly guilty.

"Well, while we're on the topic, I have kind of been meaning to ask," Emmy started, garnering looks of horror from both Violet and Yvonne. Neither girl seemed prepared for a serious discussion about the fall of their friendship. "Is Tanner, like… huge? I mean, he has to be, right?"

The release of pressure inside both Yvonne and Violet was practically audible as their tension eased. Though, for Violet, it was short-lived. While the anxiety drained, she was suddenly filled with embarrassment.

"What?" Violet didn't even know how to respond. She thought back to the note Emmy had tossed at her questioning Xander's hardware earlier that year. It wasn't welcome, but certainly a more normal way to ask this question. What could she have meant by "he has to be"?

"Oh, come on," Emmy teased, falling back into a semi-normal pattern of speech.

Violet's eyes narrowed in confusion. "'Come on' what? What do you mean? Is this one of those weird things about big feet?" She thought back to the last time Tanner walked in her direction and tried to focus his memory on his feet. They seemed normal in her head.

"Are you kidding? No! He's got a *massive* bulge. I can see it from a mile away," Emmy exclaimed.

Violet turned her eyes to Yvonne. By this point, she was looking back, nodding.

"Yeah, it's... sizeable," Yvonne commented in a hesitant whisper.

Then, the embarrassed flush that settled over her cheeks turned into a flush of rage.

How could they notice something like that about her boyfriend? It wasn't their business. It couldn't be that noticeable to other people. They had to have been looking, or worse, talking about it. They were right, he was relatively large, larger than Xander for sure, but she certainly wasn't going to say those words aloud in a crowded classroom.

She grew more frustrated. Her lips tightened into a flat line as she looked down at the table, fists balled beneath the table.

Finally, Ms. Elliot spoke up, redirecting the class into the assignment at hand. Emmy seemed to pick up on the fact that the topic was unwelcome. She must have imagined she'd jumped back into her old habits a little too quickly for Violet's comfort and simply left it alone for once.

When the period came to a close, Violet crowded out the door with the majority of the class, shouldered and elbowed her way through the crowd to be the first to exit the classroom and took off in the direction of the locker she shared with Tanner.

As she rounded the corner of the West Hall, she noticed Tanner closing the door and heading down in her direction. He spotted her quickly, waving and heading to meet her halfway.

While he walked, Violet let her eyes travel down slightly to assess the way he looked in his pants. It was a simple pair of jeans. Not particularly skinny or baggy, and at the top of his inseam rested a small hill of denim and metal zipper teeth, and somehow, seeing how blatantly obvious his bulge was didn't make her feel better about Emmy and Yvonne's comments. In fact, it made it so much worse.

How had she not noticed? It seemed too obvious. This was her boyfriend. She spent an almost immeasurable amount of time with him; their first one-on-one interaction with each other was faking a hand job just over that same bulge, and she never realized how prominent of a feature it really was.

What was wrong with her? Why couldn't she recognize these things? It seemed so stupid and silly to her that she bothered her so much. Why should she care? But then again, why did they?

Tanner's face dropped and he rushed at her, wrapping both arms around her and pressing her head onto his shoulder as they stood in the middle of the hallway, surrounded by the faceless blurs of unknown students, strangers moving around them, each in their own hurry to get where they needed to go.

That's when Violet realized the wet streams slowly coasting over the slope of her cheeks.

She was crying.

CHAPTER TWENTY-SIX

It's me.

Something is wrong with me.

Tanner held onto Violet tightly while she dampened his shoulder with her tears. She wasn't sobbing, she wasn't sad. She was frustrated.

It just didn't make any sense to her. It wasn't fair. She was so sick and tired of being disappointed and feeling so isolated, even in her own relationship. Even as Tanner held her, she couldn't help but feel cold and separate.

I'm broken.

He won't want to be with someone like me.

No one will.

This is the deal breaker.

I can't fake this forever.

I'll always be like this, and I can't be fixed.

His voice came from far away, as if at the end of a long tunnel, though he whispered it directly into her ear. "What's wrong?"

Violet shook her head in response, feeling the waffle texture of his favorite hoodie rubbing against the skin on her forehead, reminding her that she wasn't actually at the bottom of the deep, dark hole. "I'm fine," she said, her voice breaking slightly as the words came.

"Come on," he said, moving away slightly, but keeping his hands at the small of her back. He pressed his lips between her eyebrows and continued, "Let's go get some shakes or something." She was thankful he was able to understand she wasn't ready to talk. Violet wasn't certain she knew what to say yet. All the hostile phrases and self-hatred pounded against her head, trying to get out, but she knew it would only make matters worse to have to say them audibly.

Tanner led her away, down the hallways and out the door as she inhaled deep, vibrating breaths. As they moved through the parking lot to Violet's car, she handed her keys off to him.

He grabbed them without another word and slipped into the driver's seat, adjusted the mirrors and prepared to take off.

The local Shake Shoppe was only just around the corner. The outdoor seating was filled with parents and toddlers, happily coated in sticky layers of ice cream.

Tanner parked the car slowly and looked at Violet before opening the door. "Do you want to go inside?" he asked.

"Yeah," Violet sniffed, pushing the passenger side door open, and stepping out quickly. She had just peaked at her bloodshot eyes in the side mirror, ultimately deciding that this was as good as it would get without sitting in the car for another ten minutes. Tanner shuffled up behind her, lacing his fingers between hers, wordlessly opening the glass door with a large bell tied to the push-bars.

The bell clanged, alerting the employees of a new set of customers, but luckily no one seemed to pay them much attention. Tanner walked straight up to the counter and greeted the cashier.

"Hi, can I get one medium chocolate, and one medium strawberry shake?" he asked with a smile.

Violet felt like a small child, hiding behind a parent in the line at a bank. Tanner paid the cashier and ushered Violet over to a small corner booth, as private as this public location could be, and sat across from her.

He never let go of her hands, stroking his thumbs across the tops of her hands.

Throughout all of this, Violet felt as though she had been slowly dissociating. Somehow, she was both living this moment and watching it happen from a few feet away.

"Do you want to talk about it?" Tanner finally said in the silence of waiting for their shakes to be served.

Violet's lips parted, unsure of how to proceed.

"I," she started and stopped, choking over the syllables hoping to pour from her mouth. "I'm afraid," she admitted, "that you'll be mad."

Tanner cocked his head to one side. There was no face of dread or anxiety, only concern for her. "What would I be mad about? Did *I* upset you?" he asked.

She shook her head quickly, "No!" She closed her lips quickly, afraid that if she kept it open, her thoughts would start leaking out, but it was too late. The dam had already been broken.

"Idon'tlikehavingsex," her words projectiled out, occupying the space between them. They were so jumbled, it took Tanner a second to comprehend.

"What?" he asked, incredulously.

"Okay, but I don't hate it either," she continued, a little more comprehensively.

"I don't understand," Tanner said, his hands still holding hers, though a little more limply, and less assured.

Violet sighed, taking her hands away from him and pressing them to her temples. "Me either, what's why I'm so, just... frustrated, I guess?" She still couldn't quite find the right combination of words, but as they came out, this giant weight of guilt and lies spread out on the table before them like a tube of toothpaste, once full to the brim, completely emptied into a mess that couldn't be put back quite in the way it once was.

"Am I," Tanner began, choosing his words carefully, "bad at it?"

"No, no, no," Violet felt her anxiety bubbling over again as she reached back for his hands. This is exactly what she was afraid of, being misunderstood. "I just don't… care?" she offered, praying internally to anyone who was listening that he would just understand what she meant.

Tanner nodded slowly, a furrow between his brow prominent.

"Order for Tanner!" the cashier called from behind the counter, holding two medium shakes, piled high with whipped cream and bright red, shiny cherries.

He pushed off his knees to get out of his seat and grab the cups to return to the table.

Violet's breathing was fast, mocking her heartbeat pounding so hard she could hear it in her ears. If there were any self-deprecating comments floating between them now, they were absolutely drowned out by the blood pumping through her veins, fluid and warm. Her hands naturally gravitated to her hair,she absent-mindedly started twisting and untwisting the blond strands with increasing vigor, nearly to a point of tearing it out, before Tanner turned back.

She watched as he sat back down, setting her strawberry milkshake in front of her, and sitting down with his own. He hadn't taken a sip yet, but Violet jumped at the opportunity to do anything with her mouth that wasn't sticking her foot in deeper.

"So," Tanner again, spoke slowly and intentionally, "what does that mean for us?" His question was fair, innocent even.

"I could ask you the same thing," Violet replied to his question with the same. "You obviously, you know, want to," she struggled, not wanting to make assumptions. Some part of her, deep down, hoped he'd say he understood and he didn't really care about sex either, but she knew that wasn't the case.

"And you don't?" he spoke, looking her in the eyes, possibly looking for some crack to let him into her mind.

"I don't hate when we do," she clarified again. "It's just not... my favorite thing." She considered the appropriate comparison to make, and for some regrettable reason, she went with the first one that came to mind. "It's like a chore," she winced at her own words. "Like, cleaning the garage with my dad. It's big and intimidating to me, right?" Tanner nodded, following along, "But when it's done, I feel good! Like a job well done. It's satisfying, but I don't exactly get excited about it. Does that make any sense?" she asked, desperately, hoping her last few words made up for calling sex with him a "chore".

"No, I get it... I think." Tanner finally wrapped his lips around the straw and began sucking on his shake. The pressure releasing from the straw was the first noise that came from their table in a few terribly long seconds. They both seemed to struggle coming up with their next words.

"Is it just me?" Tanner finally asked. His expression demonstrated a deep frown and a few lines in his forehead following the pattern of his mouth, as though this thought had just come crashing upon him.

Violet shook her head. "No, I don't think I've ever really *wanted* to do it." For the first time, her explanation felt a little more freeing than damning as she said, "I just thought I was supposed to want it, and when I didn't, I guess I panicked and, I don't know... over-corrected." This was it, finally all the cards were on the table. The next move had to be his.

"I don't want to break up," he announced, loudly, as if to assure her that's not what he was considering. Truly, it was a bit of a relief for her. Her heartbeat relaxed a little while she impulsively sipped the remaining strawberry shake through her straw. The cup was emptied a little too quickly.

"Me either," she said, peeking into the cup to scrape the whipped cream into a ball and fish out her cherry with her straw. She gave a half-hearted laugh, hoping to lighten the mood. "I guess I should have asked for a large."

Tanner smiled back, but said nothing, starting a long slurp on his shake.

"So," she started, "you're really okay with all of this?"

Tanner released the suction on his straw again, and opened his mouth to reply, "Sort of, I mean," he dropped his cup back on the table, "it's just kind of hard to think you're not really attracted to me like that when I'm definitely into you that way." He took another sip. "Just, while we're being honest."

Violet understood, though she felt stricken with guilt. That's a fair thing to be upset about, but she never really felt that attraction to anyone. That seemed like the right thing to say, "I get that, it's just… I've never really felt that attraction to anyone. I don't just look at guys and think, like, 'Oh, yeah, he's hot. I totally want to bone him!'"

Tanner snorted a little, and covered his mouth to stop from spitting a mouthful of melted shake at his girlfriend. "Bone?"

His laugh eased her a little more, she smiled back, clarifying, "I'm serious though. I mean, even with the last guy." she didn't feel right saying Xander's name, although they were still friends and she was certain Tanner knew, there was no reason to make the conversation even more uncomfortable. "I just did it because it felt safe. I know him and I trust him, and I was trying to figure some stuff out," she waved her hands in a circular motion around her. "All this," she explained in reference to this strange admission in the corner booth of the Shake Shoppe. "He was obviously in it for different reasons, I'm sure," she spoke, perhaps a bit too candidly.

"Yeah, we don't need to talk about him," Tanner said, finally reaching the bottom of his shake as well.

Violet nodded quickly. "Of course, you're right. I'm sorry." It was time to quit while she was ahead.

"It's okay," he said, reaching his hands back across the table. She reached hers to him and they wrapped their fingers around one another's. "I don't think this has to be a big deal. I love you, Vi, and I think we can work through this." He smiled, having said a phrase that Violet hadn't even considered.

Love? Did she love him back? Was now really the time to consider it?

Quit while you're ahead, her own voice echoed, knocking at the back of her eyeballs.

"I love you too," she spoke in an almost whisper. They each stretched their necks over the plateau of the table between them, punctuating it with a sweet peck of the lips before returning to the more comfortable position across from each other.

"We should spend some time at your place after dinner on Valentine's day," she smiled, looking up at him through her eyelashes with an air of flirtation. "It's a special occasion after all."

Tanner perked up immediately, having understood the coded implication. "If you insist," he commented. Finally, he grabbed the two empty milkshake containers off the table, and slinked away to toss them in the trash a little further down the wall.

CHAPTER TWENTY-SEVEN

LINDSEY
It's my BIRTHDAY! Saturday night, pack your bags and meet at Trav's place for cake, ice cream, and a few rounds of games ;) See y'all there!

Violet reviewed the text in her bedroom, peeking in the mirror to assess her party-going outfit. High-waisted jeans and a purple cropped tank top which she made more appropriate by throwing a thick white cardigan over top. She really only kept tops like this for parties, her belly-button, she thought, was not her best quality.

She yanked a tight pair of white ankle boots over her feet and assessed herself one more time, kicking the boots up behind her to compare the slightly dirtied white to the still crisp white of the new cardigan. They were close enough; there was no time to scrub her boots perfectly clean.

She wrapped her cardigan around her tightly and galloped down the stairs, swiping her keys from the kitchen table where she'd left them and calling a goodbye to her father, eating a reheated bowl of pasta at the counter.

"You sure you don't want to stay and help me finish taking down the Christmas lights?" Mr. Gray teased.

Violet forced a laugh, saying, "I'm good, Dad. Thanks though."

In the garage, she sidestepped her way around a stack of boxes that had recently materialized a little too close to the door and made her way out to her car in the driveway. The lights were half covering the roof pieces, with the ends of the strands that still hung on blowing in the wind, or dangling at gravity's mercy.

She only had one passenger to pick up, Tanner. She'd already checked with Emmy.

VIOLET
Did you need a ride?

EMMY

No actually. Yv is taking me, she got
her mom's car for the night.

VIOLET

Gotcha

EMMY

Thanks tho! Ill see you there!

So Yvonne would be in attendance this time.
She wondered if that meant her relationship with
Steven was officially done. She couldn't imagine a
scenario where Yvonne had access to her mother's car
for the night and didn't use it to go and see her elusive
lover from a few towns over.

Instead, Violet headed to the other side of
town, where she could pull up into Tanner's house
and bring him along. It felt strange to be going to
another party in the same place their relationship
began, but this time together.

He quickly fell into her passenger seat,
angling himself over the center console to give her a
kiss. He'd been relatively happy since their
Valentine's dinner; Violet tried to pretend she didn't
notice how giddy he seemed after she'd conceded to
another dedicated evening of intimate activities.

Regardless of her thoughts about it, the happiness seemed a bit infectious for her.

They arrived relatively early compared to the collection of fashionably late friends that Violet typically fell in with Emmy as her party-going companion. Once they'd descended the steps into the basement, the room was pounding with music that seemed a bit too loud for the small group assembled there, including Lindsey, wearing a gaudy plastic "Birthday Girl" crown, Travis at her side, rolling his eyes as he rearranged the bowls of snacks, likely at Lindsey's request, Xander, sitting in a chair observing the scene, and two of Lindsey's closest friends sharing a large can of what appeared to be a warm Lime-a-Rita.

"Hey!" Violet called at Xander in the corner and immediately went to sit beside him with Tanner following. Neither Violet nor Tanner knew exactly when the rest of their little group would arrive, so Tanner naturally followed Violet to sit beside her.

"Hey, how was your dinner?" Xander asked, looking between both Violet and Tanner

"Good! The chef spanked our steak in front of us, and then he told it to call him 'daddy'," Violet replied with a laugh. Tanner only nodded.

"Sounds like a good time," he noted with his classic, natural smile.

Just then, a series of stomping footsteps came barreling into the room from the stairs. It was Emmy with Yvonne following closely behind and a couple other girls holding a set of balloons and cookies. "Happy Birthday!" the group screamed, crowding around Lindsey as she screamed and jumped with excitement at the attention.

Quickly, the noise settled as everyone fanned out in the room, heading to their go-to spots during these game nights.

Tanner tapped on Violet's shoulder. "Hey, why don't we go sit with Emmy and them?" he asked. "Just until Neil gets here, maybe?"

Violet glanced over at Emmy, taking a swig from the single, shared can of sugary booze before revealing her own wine cooler which she usually slipped from her dad's dedicated alcohol fridge in the garage when he went in for his morning bathroom time.

"Why?" Violet wondered, turning back to Tanner who looked slightly uncomfortable.

He shrugged. "I guess it doesn't matter, I just thought you'd want to say hi," he answered, obviously covering up his true intentions.

"I'll say hi a little later," she said, shrugging it off.

As the party picked up, the majority of the guests were circled around the room, including Neil. Mark and Dani insisted they would come a little later, leading Lindsey to stand up ready to announce the official start of their game.

"All right, it's *my* birthday and I didn't feel like prepping for any Truth or Dare, so tonight we're starting with Never Have I Ever, and we'll see where the evening goes from there," she exclaimed with a taste of mischief lingering in the air after her words. "Ten fingers up, first round should be the tame stuff, second round we'll start gettin raunchy, third round… well, if you're still in by the third round, you should probably come to more of these parties," she smirked. "You're out when all ten fingers are down, then you don't have to keep trying to think of things you've never done. I know for some of you whores, it'll be hard," Lindsey chuckled looking pointedly in the direction of one of her friends, giggling in the way girls do when they think they're drunk after their first time sipping on anything moderately alcoholic. "Trav, you wanna start?" she asked, turning her eye to his direction on her left.

"Sure," he said, propping his ten fingers up so everyone could see. "Never have I ever been on the freshman baseball team," he spoke confidently.

"Oh, don't be that guy," his friend Ryan groaned, putting his finger down as a result of the pointed attack.

"But that's what makes it fun!" Travis laughed, taking a fat gulp of cola from his can.

"Fine," Ryan said, now with only nine fingers to speak of. "Never have I ever hit a dog with my car," he announced, giving Travis a set of narrowed eyes.

Travis put his finger down, and incidentally, so did Yvonne.

"What?" Emmy cried, drawing attention to her dropped finger.

"It came out of nowhere," Yvonne confessed quickly. Emmy stared in horror, before the defensive shouts continued, "It survived!"

This was the natural course of the game. Things always started slightly innocent, or at least attempted to, but somewhere in the first round, someone made a pointed attack and Lindsey loved to stir the pot a little too much to stop it early.

On Violet's turn, she had all ten fingers remaining still. "Never have I ever broken a bone," she said. Several fingers went down with mutters of praise for a good, innocent, knock-out blow.

Tanner, to her left, held up eight fingers, having dropped one for a broken bone, and one for traveling out of the country. "Never have I ever had braces," he said.

The round ended with relative ease, with at least one full hand up on everyone. Some lucky souls still hovered around nines and tens.

When the next round began, Violet felt as though she actually had to pay a little attention. Up until recently, her romantic experiences had been rather minimal, now she genuinely risked getting out.

"Never have I ever had sex in a movie theatre," Travis announced.

"Bullshit," a fake-drunk girl called from a few bodies down. "Oral counts!"

Lindsey's mouth gaped open as she leaned over and smacked the girl in the leg.

"Ouch!" she cried, trying to hit her back, but missing.

"Fine, fine," Travis rolled his eyes, "Never have I ever done it in public."

Violet was surprised to see a few fingers go down.

"Never have I ever gone skinny dipping with strangers," Ryan said next.

Violet had never even gone skinny dipping with friends.

"Never have I ever slept with my ex," the next person noted. Violet felt her eyes instinctively flit to Xander, who also happened to be looking at her. They both dropped a finger. It was weird when she recalled that their entire sexual relationship took place outside of their actual relationship.

Violet noticed Tanner looking at her as she dropped her fingers, but quickly turned away when she looked at him.

"Never have I ever sent a nude," another girl chirped, making a point of scanning all the fingers that dropped for who knows what reason.

Once again, Violet removed a finger so only six remained. This time Tanner looked at her and kept his eyes firmly on her.

He hadn't been on the receiving end of those images, and he seemed to be picking up on an uncomfortable pattern that Violet was going to great lengths to avoid.

In an attempt to distract herself from the less than pleasant gaze of her boyfriend, she considered what she might say. Suddenly, she felt like there was a lot she could say. There were tons of *Cosmo* sex tips she avoided with a ten-foot pole. There was using toys, nipple stuff, and bringing food into the bedroom, but how many people around her had done that? She considered which would do the most damage, and not attract too much attention to a single individual.

She had one idea.

She still hadn't really ever masturbated. She considered it, but always found something else she'd rather be doing. She thought she'd easily knock a couple of the guys down with that one and smirked, pleased with her next words, hoping no one else would get to that before her.

Finally, at her turn, she confidently said, "Never have I ever masturbated."

A couple of scoffs and laughs came before a brief, confusing silence. Almost every finger in the room went down, more than she expected. Her stomach took no time twisting into an uncomfortable knot.

"What?" Lindsey asked from across the room. "There's no way." She looked incredulous as did many of the faces around hers.

"I straight up don't believe you, that's like saying you've never watched porn. *Everyone* has watched porn, even if it's by accident," a different girl called.

"Well," Violet said. She attempted to swallow, but it seemed to get caught on something in her throat. "I haven't," she finished her sentence, feigning as much confidence as she could manage.

"Damn, Xander was that good, huh?" Travis chuckled, stirring the pot, as he and his nosy girlfriend did. Though to Violet, it felt a bit more like setting off a whirlpool.

"Never have I ever flashed someone," Tanner called quickly, distracting the crowd from their awkward chuckles in response to Travis's comment.

The whirlpool had only begun, but it seemed too strong for him to handle.

CHAPTER TWENTY-EIGHT

The game continued. By the end of the second round, whole hands had dropped, and a few were even out completely, slightly separated from the circle so the remaining players could easily see who they'd need to skip.

Lindsey groaned as her loud-mouth friend announced on her turn, "Never have I even given oral in the movie theatre," to make up for Lindsey's little lie earlier. "Or received!" she added, making sure to nail Travis too.

Violet was stimulated in one too many ways. She felt Tanner's gaze drilling into the left side of her head, her hands were cold and clammy from the newfound anxiety that came from her mistake in announcing her masturbation habits (or lack thereof), and her face was hot from the embarrassment of having her sexual history brought up in the presence of her current boyfriend. Deep in her gut, the discomfort swirled in circles, a maelstrom of panic and anxiety. It seemed to her these parties used to be way more fun. Things had changed so much in so little time.

Lindsey, by this point, was obviously embarrassed in her own right. It made sense to Violet that she might take the quickest opportunity to get the group off her back and piling on someone else. Violet couldn't help but worry she was going to be that target.

Her stomach flipped as Lindsey's eyes met hers from across the circle with the unmistakable grin of the mean girl from every Disney Channel Original movie.

She imagined the different levels of sweating. Her palms felt like the moist, humid atmosphere of a rainforest. She stretched her fingers out slightly to hopefully cool them a little. Was it possible Lindsey could tell she was nervous from her open palm displaying her two remaining fingers?

It seemed plausible that she could. Dogs have great noses; they ought to be able to smell anxiety, and man, was she a bitch.

"Never have I ever had a friend with benefits," she sneered.

Violet and Xander dropped their fingers simultaneously. Any dirty thing she did, he'd done as well. They were both each other's firsts and she was suddenly aware that *everyone* in this basement seemed to know that.

"Never have I ever considered an electric toothbrush a sex toy," Travis piled on quickly.

Violet's eyes flashed to him. "I didn't consider it a sex toy! I never even used it!" she called, absolutely drenched in sweat and embarrassment. She jumped to her own defense probably a bit too quickly.

From the corner of her eye, she could see Tanner's visibly red face.

Xander calmly put a finger down, avoiding eye contact with Violet or his friend. "Dude, come on," he attempted to ease the attack.

"Never have I ever fucked in the parking lot at the baseball fields," the next voice called, banking on an easy detail from the rumors that, luckily for him, was profoundly true.

Violet dropped both hands in her lap, defeated, while a chorus of giggles and laughs echoed around her. The rumors seemed to come back to hurt her more than she imagined. It was one thing to know they existed, but it was a whole new situation to have them thrown in her face in the name of "good natured fun" or "just a game." It sure didn't feel like fun to her.

"You want to get out of here? We could probably just walk to my place," Violet overheard Neil asking Tanner, when she turned to them, Neil looked concerned, but there was something in his face that appeared almost pleased.

"Kind of," Tanner confessed, putting his hands on the floor to get out of his sitting position.

Neil, with the closest thing to a smile Violet had ever seen, stood beside him and claimed, "This is lame. We're heading out," as he and Tanner each grabbed their jackets from the stack on a nearby couch.

"Happy birthday, Lindsey." Tanner faked a positive tone and smile. Lindsey replied with a chirp of gratitude as she watched her chaos unfold. "See you, Vi," he said, a little quieter.

Violet stood up quickly with a hushed "Wait," escaping her lips and she followed him around the corner leading to the stairs, partially out of view to the rest of the party. She knew they would be listening.

"Can we talk for just a minute?" She tried not to sound like she was begging; she wanted to be casual and a little less embarrassing than it felt as she reached and gripped his hand in hers.

"Um," Tanner said, looking over his shoulder at an expectant Neil, "Maybe tomorrow, alright?" He gave her hand a quick squeeze before letting her go and following his friend out to the front door. She didn't move until she heard the door click.

He really left her, and she probably deserved it.

Without really looking back at anyone, expectantly waiting on her next move, Violet curled the lapel of her jacket into her fist and took off up the staircase without another word. Those people didn't deserve it.

She felt herself slamming the front door harder than was probably necessary, but she couldn't help herself. She thought about Emmy and Yvonne just sitting there, and Tanner ditching her, and Neil's subtle, smug, satisfied smile at seeing her hurt, winning a small battle for Tanner's attention.

She stood for a moment on the stoop past the front door, checking to see how far Tanner and Neil were down the street. They sauntered down the street like a pair of moonlit silhouettes, not a detail noticeable.

Violet remembered her car was in the other direction and rushed quickly and quietly to her car, nearly slipping on a patch of ice. She caught herself just in time, reaching for her door handle for balance.

The seat heaved as she dropped into it, the weight of her problems dragging her down deeper into it.

She considered going home, but she didn't want to be alone. Unfortunately for her, the majority of her friends were at the party she just left, or walking in the snow in the opposite direction.

Thankfully, she always had at least one person to count on.

VIOLET
You busy?

Luckily her reply came fast.

JESS
Just at home working on GSA stuff.
Why?

VIOLET
Rough night. Can I come over?
JESS
Always :)

Within fifteen minutes, Violet was wrapped in a blanket on Jess's floor. Though she felt like it, she didn't cry this time. She'd resolved to say she was out of tears.

Her phone buzzed with a message in a group chat she hadn't used in while. Emmy had sent a message to both her and Yvonne.

EMMY
Just checking in, V. Are you okay?

Violet chose to ignore it.

Jess came into the room with two mugs, one with hot chocolate sporting a mound of whipped cream that looked ready to topple over any second, and the other with a peppermint tea bag draped over her edge.

Violet reached for the tea, and sipped immediately. The tea scalded the roof of her mouth; she could scarcely taste the tea, but it instantly settled her stomach at least a fraction.

"What now?" Jess asked, sipping straight from her cup, letting the whipped cream form a strange mustache that started at her lip and reached just past the top of her nose.

"I don't know. I don't even know what I did to make Lindsey turn on me like that, I always thought we were good. Not friends exactly, but cool," Violet huffed, trying to cool the inside of her cheeks.

Jess listened carefully, as always.

Violet scoffed at the abrupt memory of Neil's nearly undetectable smirk. "You should have seen Neil's face, it was like he won the damn lottery." Her eyes rolled as she sighed, blowing on her tea so it might hurt a little less the second sip. It didn't hurt any less, and she didn't care much either.

"You know, it really sounds like he's jealous of you, Vi," Jess commented, prompting a quizzical face from Violet as she contemplated the possibility.

"Maybe, but why? It's not like I'm his new gaming buddy, or whatever," she groaned.

"I don't know, but whatever it is, I don't think it's really about you, I think it's about Tanner. Rumors are rough, but that seems like a serious overreaction if he just doesn't like you or your personality," she insisted.

Violet nodded, no longer wanting to talk about it. She wanted a distraction. "So what are you working on now?" she asked, turning her head to her desk to see if anything was legible from her spot on the ground.

"Well," Jess shrugged, pushing a stray braid behind her ear. "The petition failed. Principal Mick said even with the student support, the parent support is another story. Of course, I asked how he got that information and if he'd actually surveyed the parents on this, or if he was just assuming. He glossed right over that and started 'acknowledging how disappointed I must be', and how he 'sees my frustration'," she emphasized the points with one-handed air quotes, wrapping both hands around her cocoa as she finished speaking. "So I told Ms. Elliot, screw it, let's plan our first meeting for Wednesday using our loophole," she said.

"Wednesday?"

"Yup, so I've just been editing the templates you made, thanks by the way," she added that aside before continuing, "and also I've been coming up with the meeting agenda. I want it to be pretty informative, so I'm trying to do a PowerPoint. I also really don't want to get anything wrong, so I'm really going hard on all the research, and," she seemed to be getting lost in her mental to-do list, before catching herself and looking back at Violet, "now I'm taking a break."

Violet smiled and held out her mug of tea for Jess to tap her mug against, silently toasting their friendship and taking a deep gulp of their respective beverages.

She felt so much warmer then.

CHAPTER TWENTY-NINE

VIOLET

Can we talk now?

TANNER

Sure.

VIOLET

Are you mad?

TANNER

Should I be? It was all in the past,

right?

VIOLET

You seemed mad last night...

TANNER

Maybe a little, but I guess I can't

really be mad. It's not like any of this

happened when we were talking…

right?

VIOLET

Not even a little bit! I'm so so sorry

any of that was brought up. Xander

  probably told Travis who told
Lindsey. I didn't even know they
knew about those things.

TANNER

Its just weird since everything I've
ever done is with you, and you have
a whole history of things you've
never done with me.

          VIOLET

I get that. I mean, is there anything
you really wanted to try that we've
never done? I guess I never asked.

TANNER

The pictures made me a little
jealous... and kind of worried. What if
he still has them?

          VIOLET

He doesn't. Xander's trustworthy and
he's always been a good friend. He
wouldn't keep anything like that,
especially if I asked him to delete
them, which I did. Immediately after
they were sent.

TANNER

Right...

          VIOLET

I can do a little photoshoot for you
tonight... if you want? I can make it
special for you. :)

TANNER
Well, if your offering Im not gonna
refuse :)

VIOLET
you're*. ;)

Violet reread the conversation that Sunday night as she dressed herself in a bright-blue thong *only*. She couldn't help but think how her aunt was the one to pick this out for her. It wasn't that Mr. Gray was uncomfortable with getting lady's undergarments for his daughter, it's more so that he was afraid he'd get the wrong ones. He always enlisted the help of his sister to pick out new panties and bras for Violet every year around Christmas so she'd have some for the next year. Her aunt's assistance was something Violet was grateful for as well. For some reason, she imagined getting lost in the underwear section, not knowing what to purchase, and she definitely didn't want to have to go underwear shopping with her dad—it was his money, after all.

It also somehow put her in a strange position of having underwear she never once expected to have, which included this electric blue, lacy thong. It was itchy, slightly too big for her, and mildly uncomfortable, but she really only needed it for her photoshoot.

This blue was Tanner's favorite color.

She stood a couple feet in front of her full-length mirror and posed. She considered putting on heels, per a saucy tip from *Cosmo* about taking appealing nudes, but it seemed so inauthentic.

She angled the phone down and took a few full-body shots without her head in them. She couldn't bring herself to include her face ever.

She sent one more text to be safe before sending the pictures.

VIOLET
Are you alone? :)

TANNER
Yes :)

She sent the first one, and as she waited for a response, she slipped into a far more comfortable pair of bikini briefs, sports bra, and a pair of thick athletic shorts. She didn't like to be naked all too long. She curled up in a blanket on her bed and waited.

TANNER
Send more, please :)

Violet smiled and sent her next picture to him. She always liked to take a couple pictures and send them slowly like she was taking them as she talked.

What Tanner didn't know wouldn't hurt him.

And feeling satisfied that she'd dug herself out of the uncomfortable hole she found herself in the night before, she decided it was time to go to bed after one last text.

VIOLET
Delete those, please :) And I'll see
you tomorrow.

* * *

Violet floated her way through the lunch line Monday afternoon. She usually packed a lunch, but she found herself dreading coming back to the school to find out if she'd be the topic of any new gossip. As a result, she slept in just a touch so she'd be a few minutes late to school and could enjoy the peace and quiet as she walked to her math class in an empty hallway. Old habits die hard, apparently, as she still rushed around the house with the attitude of someone who did *not* intend to be late, and tripped over a set of Christmas lights Mr. Gray had yet to roll up neatly in the garage, resulting in what would certainly be a fat bruise on her right butt cheek later. The mess in the garage had simply gotten out of control.

She gripped the sides of her styrofoam tray and peeked around the corner out of the lunch buffer, eying her table from across the room. She hadn't spoken to Tanner in person yet, but she was hoping to see him in a good mood today. Just over a couple of heads, Violet could make out the shape of Dani's gravity defying pixie cut, but not Tanner yet.

"Move," someone growled from behind her in the lunch line. She was blocking the exit.

"Sorry," she said, quickly shifting out of her current position and heading over to her table.

"Violet?" a voice asked from behind after a few steps. It was familiar, and surprising. She turned to look.

It was Yvonne.

Violet straightened herself a little, and replied, "Yeah, what's up?" It felt fake coming from her mouth, but it was too late to stuff it back inside.

"Um, I just wanted to ask if you're doing okay? After Saturday, I mean. You didn't respond to Emmy's message," she spoke quietly. She looked almost bashful. Maybe ashamed? Violet couldn't quite put a finger on it, but there was certainly something different about this interaction compared to the other rare chats they've had in the past few months.

"I'm fine," Violet finally said. "Lindsey's just a bitch."

Yvonne couldn't stop herself from snorting a little, and honestly, Violet began laughing too. It had been a while since Violet had just let her first thought slip, and it felt surprisingly freeing knowing anyone around her could have heard. Part of her really hoped it got back to Lindsey; she deserved to know.

"I also just wanted to say that I'm sorry?" Her apology sounded more like a question, wondering before she gave it if it would be accepted.

"For what?" Violet replied like she didn't know, but really she wanted to know what specifically she was sorry for; a. Calling her a slut, b. Not apologizing sooner, or c. Being a bad friend to her, or d. All of the above.

"For everything," Yvonne replied.

Ding, ding! Correct, Violet thought, but she listened patiently.

"I broke up with Steven," she said. "It's weird to say, but I think he kind of turned me against you guys. I never spent any time with you guys because he said I should *want* to spend more time with him, and you guys saw me every day. I got excited at the idea of us double-dating with him and Derek and when you weren't interested, Derek got pissed, and Steven got pissed and they just said so much bad stuff about you... I don't know, I started to believe it, and that's just not fair," Yvonne confessed, her eyes darting in every direction but Violet's.

"He finally talked me into sleeping with him and I felt nothing but anger and regret; I had to break up with him as soon as possible. I sent him this big, long text. It was more like a novel, if we're being honest. He blew up my phone all night, called me tons of names."

Violet continued to listen, not giving any indication if she would accept or reject her apology.

"You're not a slut. It was a terrible, stupid thing for me to say, and Xander's a good guy. He was willing to defend you in a room full of people. I couldn't even defend you to my one shitty boyfriend. And you and Tanner are so good together. You just seem so happy and I'm happy for you, and... I just want you to know that. I get it, and I'm sorry I was so… judgy," she struggled with that last word.

Violet smiled softly, and looked down at her lunch, forming grease pools in the corners of the white styrofoam.

"Where've you been eating?" Violet asked, looking back up. "Our table's been empty." She motioned her head to the desolate table beside the wide, brick support column.

"Honestly, I've just been switching between teacher's classrooms saying I needed somewhere quiet to work on homework," Yvonne said, sheepishly.

"Well, don't do that; come sit with us," Violet offered, turning off to show her table, now full with her new friends, and Neil.

Yvonne perked up instantaneously. "Sounds great!"

And she followed Violet to enjoy their first lunch together in what felt like forever.

CHAPTER THIRTY

The day, once again, came to close. Before the bell rang to usher students into their final classes of the day, Violet and Yvonne huddled close at their lab table while scrolling through the call logs on Yvonne's phone. She wanted to show Violet the series of unrelenting phone calls and voicemails Steven had left her.

He flipped like a switch, back and forth, between sweet-talking politely and calling Yvonne every name in the book for ignoring him. She held firm.

"Have you told your parents?" Violet asked, feeling fairly worried about her friend's safety.

"Yeah, they told me to just keep everything on my phone and not to delete anything so I'd have evidence if I ever need to get a restraining order," Yvonne replied.

"Hello, ladies! What have we here?" Emmy squealed, walking in to the sound of the bell. For the last week since they had started the project, she was used to coming into the classroom to find Violet and Yvonne going out of their way to avoid eye contact, let alone having a full-blown conversation within inches of each other. She dramatically pulled her glasses off and rubbed the lens on her shirt, pushing them back up her nose to reassess. "It looks to me like we're being *friendly*!" she sang sweetly.

"We ate lunch together today too," Violet pointed out, happy to feel this positive energy around her.

For the last few months, she'd felt so clouded by confusion and isolation, even when she was around others, and especially Tanner. She watched Emmy get into her usual seat, across the table from the two of them. She felt a slight smile creep across her face. That moment felt familiar, even after distancing herself from them for so long.

Emmy's smile was unbreakable, even as Ms. Elliot commanded the attention of the room.

"Good afternoon, class!" she called from her whiteboard where she was still writing some information in the top right corner.

She had paused just long enough for one table of jokesters to reply, "Good afternoon, Ms. Elliot!" in unison, issuing a tone reminiscent of a cult following.

She turned around with a fake laugh, "Ha ha," and capped her markers. "Before we get started on our presentations today, I just wanted to give a brief announcement," she said with a booming teacher-voice, garnering the attention of almost everyone aside from the student who'd already passed out on their table.

Ms. Elliot motioned to what she'd just written on the board. "The community GSA, or Gay-Straight Alliance, has just received permission to rent out a room after school on Wednesdays to host meetings. So, if any of you are interested," her eyes flashed to the table with the three girls, looking at her reassuringly, "make sure to stick around after class on Monday to get some information. Tell your friends!"

There was a wave of murmurs around the room, allowing the students to react, before Ms. Elliot continued, "Now, we will start our presentations.

Table three, you signed up first, so come on and get set up."

As table three gathered their poster together, and one student shuffled back before Ms. Elliot's desk to use her computer, Violet instinctively pulled out her phone to check it, along with everyone else.

As she expected, she had an email notification from Jess with information about the GSA.

Hello, **everyone**!

It's officially go-time!

The *community* GSA organization has finally received permission to use the school building as a meeting place. For the foreseeable future, meetings will be held on **Wednesdays**, after school in **room 429**, also known as Ms. Samantha Elliot's chemistry classroom. Ms. Elliot will be our advisor and school liaison.

This **Wednesday, February 19th**, from **2:30PM-3:30PM**, we'll have a bunch of information about the group's mission and activities to help recognize the myths and stereotypes surrounding the LGBTQ+ community!

Please, invite anyone you like, and we'll see you on Wednesday!

Sincerely,

Jess Daniels

Student Organizer

PS. There will be **snacks!**

Violet naturally tapped on the forward button and sent the information off to Tanner, Mark, Dani, and even Neil. She slipped her phone back into her pocket for easier access and refocused her attention to the front of the class. Table three was about to start their presentation.

*   *   *

At two o'clock on Wednesday, Violet scurried away from Ms. Elliot's room to do a quick exchange at her locker. That morning, her shared locker with Tanner became a shared locker with Tanner and Jess as Jess had too many materials for the GSA meeting. They simply wouldn't fit into her locker alone.

As Violet rounded the corner which hid her locker from sight, she noticed Tanner pulling things apart inside, obviously looking for something.

"Hey! What's wrong?" Violet asked, coming up a little more quickly and beginning to collect the bags of nametags and paper plates Jess had stuffed in there earlier.

"I totally forgot, my dad set up an interview for me today, and I can't find my stupid resume," Tanner groaned with his knees on the ground as he flipped through all the folders in his backpack rapidly.

"An interview? Where? Can you still come to the GSA meeting?" Violet asked, slipping the handles of the bags over her arms so she'd still have the mobility of her arms.

"No, I can't. My brother's coming to pick me up now. I don't know what it is, some restaurant a few towns over. It's in the text from my dad," his words came out quickly and thoughtlessly.

Violet noticed his phone sitting on the shelf where they normally left their notes to one another. "Can I look?" she asked, hovering her hand over his phone.

"Three-six-three-six," he replied, giving her the passcode to open the device.

She tapped the numbers, feeling the *buzz* of every number in her fingertips. The screen performed a slide animation to reveal… her?

Violet's heart sank so low, she felt like it would drop right out of her body. It was a picture of her, her mostly naked body, covered only barely by a bright blue thong. The camera cropped her head off just above the shoulders.

He told me he deleted these, she recalled silently. *He showed me*. She scanned the screen for more information until she noticed she was in his email app. She backed out of the image and noticed the email she'd sent him only two days ago with the GSA information a few messages above the ones with the pictures, marked as received from his own email account. He sent them to himself. He emailed himself copies of the images so he could delete them from his phone and show Violet that he'd done so.

And he was looking at them during school. Where anyone could see.

"Oh thank god!" Tanner sighed, untensing. "Found it." He got to his feet and noticed Violet's pale face, taking on a green tinge as if she were about to be sick. He narrowed his eyes in confusion and quickly snatched his phone back out of her hands. He must have realized just then, no-longer distracted by his resume, what Violet must have seen when she unlocked his phone.

"You said you deleted those," she said so quietly she could barely hear herself.

"I did," he answered defensively.

"But you sent them to yourself," she continued, with a hint of accusation. "I trusted you with this, and you lied to me."

Tanner looked around as if his perfectly reasonable explanation was about to come flying down the hallway; it didn't.

"Can we talk about this later, Vi? I really have to go," he slammed the locker closed and walked around her, heading off, not waiting for her response. Cowardice at its finest.

Violet turned and gripped the combination to open the locker again. She hadn't grabbed the last bag. She slipped it over her wrist before slamming the door shut, letting out a little of her aggression, and stalking back down the hallway.

Maybe her face wasn't in those pictures, but on Tanner's phone she was certain anyone who caught a glimpse would assume it was her. She felt so exposed with the idea of people seeing her completely vulnerable like that. She felt incrementally worse as she considered that Tanner might have been *showing* those images to people. Could he be so cruel and thoughtless? And what would others think when they saw the fake confidence in her body posture, as if she was showing off, or hoped to be seen in that way.

She didn't want to take those pictures. She wanted to appease him, to make him happy. She already had such a neutral view on sexual relationships, but she could feel her views becoming more and more negative by the day as she feigned her interest in them over and over to give Tanner the *normal* relationship that *he* wanted.

Even having admitted to herself and her boyfriend that she wasn't particularly interested in exploring this side of their relationship, he hadn't quite accepted her differences. That hint of pseudo-acceptance from Tanner had given her subconscious just enough confidence to reveal this part of her identity at Lindsey's party, but the instant ridicule and rejection shut her down rather quickly. She wondered, as she walked, how much Tanner really respected what she wanted, or if throwing her sexual history in her face was his way of manipulating her into going further. Or maybe, she was a terrible, horrible girlfriend for not offering these things in the first place.

What if everything was her fault? All because she just didn't feel like being intimate.

She was grateful to have the GSA meeting to distract herself.

When she re-entered Ms. Elliot's classroom, Jess was setting up snacks at the lab table where Violet worked with Emmy and Yvonne. Beside her was another student who looked sort of familiar, though Violet was certain she'd never met her before.

"I've got the plates," Violet said, mustering up as much positive tone and energy as she could manage at the time. While her energy seemed low, her tone was enough to prevent Jess from rousing any suspicion that something might have gone wrong.

"Awesome! This is Neveah, she volunteered to help set-up and tear down with us," Jess said, still hyper-focused on her hands as they worked quickly to set the table. "I'm going to pull up the PowerPoint if you two could keep unpacking here?" Jess asked, leaving the two to head to the other side of the classroom once she'd received their nods in agreement.

"I'm Violet," Violet said, performing a wobbly wave in Neveah's direction, weighed down by grocery bags.

"Hey!" she did a chin nod back. Violet again couldn't help but notice how familiar she looked.

"Have we met before? You look really familiar," Violet said, setting her bags on the table to begin unpacking them.

"Probably not, I do post-secondary classes at the community college most of my day," Neveah replied, starting to help Violet unpack. "You might know my brother though," she added.

"Who's your brother?"

"Neil Davidson?" she asked.

"Oh, wow, yeah! You two look so much alike!" Violet said in awe.

"Wait," she turned and looked at Violet more closely, "Are you Violet, like Tanner's girlfriend Violet?"

Violet swallowed, trying to avoid the thought of Tanner, "Yup, that's me," she answered.

"Got it," she said, drawing out the words. "Neil talks about you a lot," she said passively.

"Nothing good I imagine," Violet chuckled.

"Don't take it personally, he's kind of a grouch. Especially when anyone threatens his relationship with his *best friend*." Her emphasis seemed unusual.

Violet nodded slightly.

"But, he's my brother, and I love him, so I want to support him," Neveah kept speaking through Violet's silence.

"Oh," she finally replied, surprised by how candid she'd be. Was she going to be as nasty to her as her brother was just because Neil didn't like her?

"Sorry," Neveah picked up on her wariness. "Not about you. I meant with the GSA," she explained.

"Oh," Violet relaxed a little. "Oh!" she repeated, a lightbulb going off in her head. "He's gay?" Violet asked for clarification.

"Bi. Did you not know? He's pretty open about it. Then again, I'm sure he doesn't go out of his way to tell you much about himself," she reasoned, unwrapping the last package of paper plates and setting them at the edge of the table.

"He does not. I once drove him to work in complete silence," Violet chuckled at the memory. It was funny now that it wasn't so recent.

Neveah laughed with her. "That sounds about right."

CHAPTER THIRTY-ONE

The room quickly filled with students from every social group, all casually gathering snacks and forming groups with familiar faces around the lab desks.

Once the second hand finally hit the two-thirty mark, Jess wasted no time jumping right in and shushing the crowd.

Violet sat with Emmy and Yvonne in the back of the classroom. It was strange seeing Ms. Elliot from a different angle, and not teaching chemistry. Dani and Neil sat at the table just in front of them, all eyes on Jess as she spoke.

"My name is Jess Daniels; many of you probably know me as the VP of Student Council, but today I'm coming to you as the student coordinator of the new *community led* Gay-Straight Alliance," she announced. Half the room began clapping and hooting at her as she turned and motioned to Ms. Elliot. "We also have Ms. Elliot, your favorite chemistry teacher, here to act as both our advisor and a school-liaison, since again, this is *not* sponsored by the school." She and Ms. Elliot smiled as if they were in on some private joke, but even members of their audience couldn't help but chuckle at the subtle, passive aggressive, ass-covering comments Jess threw in her opening speech.

Ms. Elliot stepped forward. "I'm Ms. Elliot, and I'm really excited to see all of you here today! As a part of a different generation from yours, it makes me so happy to see such a diverse group of students coming together for support of your peers. When I was growing up and my brother came out as gay, life was very difficult for him in a community that feared what they didn't understand. The goal here is to spread tolerance and acceptance for everyone in the LGBT community and to become active participants to stand up against unfair treatments of our fellow members," she explained. The movement in the classroom was all in agreement as students nodded along with her speech.

"Today, our focus is on *information*!" Jess called, commanding attention back to her. "We want to identify the current state of the community and explore the definitions of LGBTQQIA+ for everyone's benefit. It also may help you understand a little more about yourself. So we're going to start off with the Kinsey scale. Has anyone heard of this before?"

"It gives you your gay-straight rating!" someone shouted back from one of the front tables.

"Exactly!" Jess said. "This is a short, seven question quiz that helps people describe their sexual orientation. Now, if anyone is uncomfortable with this activity, please feel free to sit out and watch. What I have here," she raised a stack of papers in her hand, "is a paper-copy of the Kinsey Scale assessment. For those of you who aren't trying to leave a paper trail, feel free to go to this website on your phones," she pointed back to the whiteboard where Ms. Elliot wrote a URL on the board. "Let's see how we identify," she said, beginning to walk toward the outstretched arms reaching for a paper copy of the test.

Violet took note of the website URL. She and her friends immediately to her left and right pulled out their phones to copy the information on the board.

https://www.idrlabs.com/kinsey-scale/test.php

Dani and Neil patiently waited for their paper copies, grabbing their pens while they waited.

The room began tapping and circling away, completing the simple math to see how they ranked on the scale.

Violet read through the first question.

To whom are you attracted?
a.　　　Both men and women.
b.　　　Mostly people of the opposite sex from mine.
c.　　　Mostly people of the same sex as mine.
d.　　　Only people of the opposite sex from mine.
e.　　　Only people of the same sex as mine.

She tapped on d, and moved on to the next question.

Who have you had sex with?

a.   Both men and women.

b.   Both men and women, but I prefer people of the opposite sex from mine.

c.   Both men and women, but I prefer people of the same sex as mine.

d.   Only people of the opposite sex from mine.

e.   Only people of the same sex as mine.

She tapped on d again. Question three.

Who have you had sexual fantasies about?

She made a face. She didn't really have sexual fantasies. If left to her own devices, and not inundated with non-stop subliminal messaging reminding her of sex, would she ever think about it? Laying alone in bed in the dark seemed like the best test, and she never once used her completely free time to fantasize about anyone.

"Some of you might be noticing", Ms. Elliot said, interrupting the train of thought and directing the attention away from the test momentarily, "that this assessment does have limitations, namely no representation for non-binary folk and the differences between romantic and sexual attraction, but just answer to the best of your ability. I promise, we'll address this shortly."

Violet nodded and continued to finish the survey, selecting responses that positively referred to the opposite sex exclusively. She submitted and page refreshed and showed a scale made of several bodies, on the far left reading "exclusively heterosexual", and on the far right reading "exclusively homosexual." A yellow box circled around the far left. That sounded right to her.

"Exclusively heterosexual," Yvonne said aloud for Emmy and Violet to hear.

"Same," Violet replied.

"Heterosexual, incidental homosexual tendencies," Emmy said with a face of interest.

"Really?" Yvonne questioned.

Emmy shrugged. "I don't know…a threesome would be cool," she said casually.

"Everyone finishing up?" Ms. Elliot asked, wandering around the room. Some verbal responses came in the affirmative.

"Awesome!" Jess exclaimed, clicking a button on a remote in her hand to reveal an image of a graph with a positive correlation, heading up and to the right to show a gradual increase. "Again, if you're uncomfortable sharing and just want to observe, feel free to stay seated, but now we're going to physically represent the spectrum so we can see the distribution here in our group today. If you scored exclusively heterosexual, head over there," she pointed to the side of the room which lined up with the starting point of the graph. "And if you score exclusively homosexual, head over there," she pointed to the side of the room lining up with the end of the graph. "If you were somewhere in the middle, fill in where you belong."

Almost everyone stood up and began filling in their positions. A fair amount of students hung around the exclusively heterosexual side of the graph, probably around half, while the remainder filtered out slowly leaving only one person at exclusively homosexual and a greater variety of students somewhere in the middle. Neil punctuated the center mark, Jess and Emmy shared a space just slightly ahead of the exclusively heterosexual mark. Dani watched from the table. Violet wondered if it was because they identified as non-binary, like Ms. Elliot noted.

Jess stepped out of line and turned to address the small crowd. "The reason we did this exercise is to demonstrate to you all that sexuality is a spectrum. Many of us don't fit in the 100% gay or straight category because sexuality isn't that simple. The idea that you have to be one or the other is simply false. You can all head back to your seats."

The crowd collected back at their tables.

"What other myths or struggles do we think the outside person might not understand about sexuality?" Ms. Elliot prompted a discussion.

"That it's static," a boy chimed in from a few tables in front of Violet.

"Great! Elaborate," Ms. Elliot pressed.

"I might identify as gay now, but maybe in a few years I'll identify as pansexual. Sexuality isn't just non-binary, it can be fluid."

"Great point, what else?" she continued, seeking out students to call upon.

"That two people can't be gay and just be friends, or, like, straight guys and girls can just be friends. It really bugs me when girls think I'm going to try and get with them just because I'm bi," a girl from the other side of the room called.

"Or when you are trying to get with someone, and you're laying it on super thick, and you don't know if they could be gay or not," another student called from the table behind her, "and you don't want to outright say you're gay or ask them because it can go *so* wrong."

"Seriously," Neil added, nodding in agreement.

Violet's eyes burned into the back of Neil's head. Was she reading too far into it, or was this finally the explanation she'd been looking for?

Was Neil into Tanner? Could that have been why he hated her so much?

Maybe Jess was right, everything he did was jealous behavior. Everything really started to click into place.

Violet then remembered to refocus on the meeting. She'd zoned out of the conversation, and quickly tried to come back in.

"That's why it's so important to ask, otherwise you'll never know. It's *never* fair to assume, regardless of your assumption," Jess was saying.

"On that note, I'd like to take the time to review our LGBTQ acronym and make sure we all understand what that means and the community we're supporting. Something else that's important to note is everything that is included in the 'plus' in LGBTQ+." She clicked a button on the remote again revealing a slide with a series of letters. She began again, "the full acronym is LGBTQQIP2SAA, and honestly, there might be more."

The room was quiet; the group listened politely and intently as Jess defined the terms.

"Most of us probably know these first five: lesbian, gay, bisexual, transgender, and queer, right?"

A chorus of yeses and yups responded.

"Awesome, so anyone know what might be our second Q?" she clicked another button on her remote, prompting a laser pointer to shoot out of it. She circled the second Q.

Violet chuckled at how much Jess seemed to be enjoying her clicker.

"Questioning?" Dani replied.

"Correct! It's important to recognize and support everyone in the community, even if they're unsure where they belong. Next is I. This means," she clicked through the slides to get to the correct one, "Intersex. Intersex is defined as anyone who is born with both male and female reproductive or sexual anatomy, thus not fitting into the gender binaries of male and female."

She continued through the next letters, "Pansexual, pan stems from the language of the Greeks, meaning all. Those who identify as pansexual simply do not limit their sexual attraction to any gender binaries or identities.

"The acronym 2S stands for two-spirit. This means those with this identity identify with both masculine and feminine *spirits*. This differs from intersex as intersex is generally focused on the physical and anatomical, while two-spirit focused more on the mental and emotional responses to masculinity and femininity. This is a wide umbrella term to encompass many people who do not feel they fit into the standard gender binary.

"Last, but certainly not the least, we have two As. Any guess on what either of these As stand for?" Jess asked.

"Allies?" Yvonne answered, her voice carrying across the classroom.

"Yes, that's one of them! Representing many of you here who came for support and appreciation. And what about that last A?" Jess looked around, waiting for an answer for a few seconds before clicking onto the next slide.

"This A is for asexual."

CHAPTER THIRTY-TWO

Violet searched her mind for a guess about what that might mean. She remembered learning about asexual plant and sea-life in biology. These were organisms which were able to reproduce on their own, almost like making a copy of themselves.

She wondered how that might be possible in humans.

"Asexuality," Jess continued, "is a lack of sexual attraction or desire, or to some people, the absence of a sexual orientation altogether." She clicked to the next slide. "Obviously, this acronym is really just an umbrella term to encompass a wide range of identities, and each of these letters hosts a plethora of subcategories which are far more likely to resonate with any of your particular preferences. The important thing here is that all of these identities are valid and that we work together to create a safe and inclusive community for everyone at Northridge High School," Jess finalized her speech and reached the end of her presentation. A few voices hooted and clapped for her as she began to exit out of the slides on Ms. Elliot's screen.

"Thank you all again for coming to our first meeting. We still have the space until three-thirty, so please feel free to hang out, get to know one another, and eat some snacks. We are planning on hosting our next meeting in two weeks. We want to present a couple of different charity organizations that assist in supporting the LGBTQ+ community and possibly do some planning for a fundraiser to raise awareness for the new club and also to raise some money for a worthy cause," Ms. Elliot explained.

"Oh, and we have tons of other things planned, like watching some documentaries and hosting round-tables with student council and school officials for the sake of starting a conversation, so if you want to help with the planning and take a bigger role in the group, please let me know! We're just starting out so we need all the help we can find!" Jess added her comments frantically as the group's attention dissipated.

The room around her moved quickly as she tried to slow her mind and focus back on what Jess had said.

The lack of sexual attraction, she repeated. *There's a name for it?*

"Hey," Dani turned in their chair to look at Violet, "Where's Tanner? I thought he was coming?"

Violet shrugged. "He had an interview last minute." Though her body language was relaxed, her voice crackled with a bitter venom.

"Woof, you okay?" Dani asked. Violet noticed Neil slightly turning to eavesdrop on their conversation as he would never want to actively participate in a conversation with Violet.

Violet laughed nervously. While she'd grown to consider Dani a friend, she still wasn't sure if they would be on her side in this particular matter, "Um," she decided to answer carefully, "we got into a bit of an argument before the meeting."

"Really? What happened?" Dani inquired, ignoring Neil turning further to pay closer attention.

Violet felt her skin darkening with the red flush of embarrassment, mixed with the burning eyes of the now engrossed Yvonne and Emmy who had originally been glancing around the room, she felt hot and a little dizzy making the announcement. Even if Dani wasn't with her, at least Emmy and Yvonne would be.

"Well," she slowed and quieted her voice, "I sent him some pictures last weekend, and I, um… found them open on his phone... after he said he deleted them."

Neil jumped to Tanner's defense rather quickly. "Why were you going through his phone?"

Violet jumped to her own defense even quicker. "I wasn't! He said I could check the texts from his dad for the place he was interviewing at and it was just there when I unlocked his phone!" she replied so quickly, she wasn't sure if it made her sound more guilty or less. She immediately questioned the details she considered important enough to include, but instead of continuing, she quieted. Tanner was the one who had done something wrong, not her. She didn't need to defend herself.

In the silence, Emmy spoke first. "What a dickhead," she said.

Violet's eyes immediately flashed to Neil's who had his eyes staring hard at her, angry.

"Actually yeah, that's a total dickhead move," Dani said. Violet didn't mind losing the staring competition to turn her attention to them.

"Agreed. Super skeezy," Yvonne added.

"I," Violet had finally relaxed enough to feel candid, even with Neil there. He could take anything she said back to Tanner and she wouldn't care. He hurt her, and she was allowed to be upset. "I don't know what to do," she finished. "He just walked away and said we could talk about it later, but honestly, I don't want to talk to him. The more I'm thinking about it, the more I just want him to stay away from me for a while."

"Then make him stay away," Dani affirmed.

Violet nodded slightly. "You really think so?" She could feel the subtext of her question slipping out, which Dani addressed immediately.

"He's my friend, and I love the guy, but that's a dick head move," they flashed their eyes to Emmy who gave a satisfied smile, "he broke your trust, now you get to choose how to go forward. If I were in your position, I would be pissed." They sipped from a styrofoam cup of a dark soda, still resting on their table. Neil didn't appear particularly upset, nor particularly chipper. Violet wondered if he was more excited at her misery or more disappointed in everyone talking badly about Tanner.

The rustling sound of paper plates and cups crashing into the base of the tiny gray trash cans one after another signaled the exit of several group members, some thanking Jess for her presentation as she folded up bags of chips and dumped extra cups of soda and lemonade down the drains at the lab table sinks.

Neveah appeared among Violet's little group huddled in the back of the classroom, holding a bag of kettle-cooked chips Jess had handed off to her as left-overs and tapped her brother on the shoulder. "You ready to go?" she asked. Looking at her was like seeing Neil smile sincerely, which gave Violet an uneasy feeling.

"Yeah," he said, pushing himself up and out of the chair, nodding at Dani directly before shuffling after his sister with his hands in his pockets.

"He creeps me out," Emmy admitted as he left earshot.

Violet shrugged; she didn't quite want to defend him, but after today she felt for a moment she understood him a little better. Though she didn't necessarily appreciate the way he interacted with her, she had maybe garnered just a little inch of sympathy for him, especially when considering that if Neil was interested in a romantic relationship with Tanner, Tanner wouldn't be reciprocating those feelings. Even if Tanner and Violet broke up, he wasn't sexually attracted to men, and as it would appear, neither was Violet.

The meeting officially ended seven minutes early when Jess and Ms. Elliot were the only people remaining in the room, feeling satisfied with what they'd done and excitedly talking about the turn-out and planning for their next meeting.

Violet waved goodbye to her friends who all filtered into their respective cars and drove away. She plopped into her driver's seat, and looked out her windshield at the mostly empty parking lot. A small portion of the lot was still full with the cars of the basketball players, practicing for their last games of the season, and one remaining vehicle housed the silhouettes of two students evidently attached at the mouth.

She turned her head in the opposite direction and started her car, but didn't shift into drive just yet. She was clearly distracted with this idea in her head, and her curiosity couldn't wait until she arrived at home.

She pulled her phone out of her back pocket, shimmying slightly in her seat so it could wiggle out. She turned the screen on and tapped on her search bar, taking note of the absence of notifications on her messaging app. Unsurprisingly, this didn't make her feel any sort of way.

"Define asexual," she typed, whispering the words slowly as each letter appeared, with no hesitation as she clicked search, anticipating the results.

asexual

noun

a person who has no sexual feelings or desires, or who is not sexually attracted to anyone.

Exactly what Jess had said. She scrolled a little further in her search results, absorbing the little details that stuck out in the subheadings of every search result.

Also known as "ace".

Different from celibacy or sexual abstinence

May still be considered straight, gay, or bi because sexual attraction is only one of many types of attraction.

Most popular asexual community: Asexual Visibility and Education Network (AVEN)

As she continued scrolling, she felt somewhat lighter. Every tid-bit she read, every line her eyes scanned, prompted that unforgiving little voice in the back of her head to scream at her.

Yes.

Yes.

Exactly.

Yes.

That's just like me.

I'm just like that.

Yes.

The next line that caught her attention had her tapping immediately. A question now tap dancing around with that voice in her brain.

How do I know if I'm asexual?

The link swapped the page of search results out for a colorful slides presentation. Her eyes drank in every bit of information they could, it was as though they had been starved for this knowledge and every line, word, and letter gave her bursts of energy to keep reading until she felt fulfilled, even happy.

Someone can still be attracted to someone even if they don't like or want to have sex. Some asexuals may still engage in sexual acts. Others may not. Being ace just means you don't *desire* sex.

Approximately 1% of people are asexual (Seventy-five MILLION people).

But the big, bolded words at the top of the next slide really hit her the hardest.

Asexuality is completely normal.

She had no concept of the time that passed as she sat in her car, scrolling through links and slides and articles. It could have been anything from a few minutes to several days as she consumed herself in this new fascinating information. Every testimonial she read boosted her confidence.

> I felt so broken for so long.
>
> It's hard to set boundaries with partners.
>
> I felt ostracized and pressured by the culture around me.

She looked up and out her window at the setting sun. It had been nearly an hour since just sitting in her car. The sun set so early in these winter months, and the darkening sky prompted her to refocus on getting home, she just hoped everything would still be there to read in the ten minutes it would take her to get home. She was almost afraid to stop looking, fearing it was all a strange dream that she would escape once she blinked and realized she'd been in bed this whole time, but that wasn't the case. Sitting there, staring into the orangey-yellow clouds, it was like floating. She strapped her seatbelt over her chest, feeling as light as she did, she didn't want to risk simply floating away.

Then she was brought back down to Earth with a harsh vibration.

TANNER
Can we talk?

CHAPTER THIRTY-THREE

Violet looked away from the screen quickly. She didn't want to talk, that much was clear to her. But, she wondered, did she owe it to him to hear him out? He was her boyfriend, after all.

Her lips tightened. It was fascinating to her that her mood could shift so quickly. She'd been ripped from Eden, a sweet place of understanding and clarity.

Instinctively, she backed out of her messages with Tanner and shifted to the group chat with Emmy and Yvonne.

What was there to say?

Tanner texted me. What do I do?

Her fingers flitted across the electronic keyboard, leaving those words etched across the bottom of her screen in preparation to send. She couldn't help but hesitate.

Do I really need to ask them?

She knew what she wanted already. Why did she need them to reassure her that this was the right choice?

The last few months, everything she did, she did it because she thought that's what she was supposed to do. Countless hours were spent stressing over her next moves and planning every interaction down to the minute to feel normal.

But I am *normal,* she recalled the bolded words informing her of that very fact only moments before.

Where was she now after following everyone else's advice? She felt so weighed down by her regrets at that moment, and she couldn't help but wonder how much of her heartbreak and drama in the past year could have been avoided if she'd only made the choice to listen to herself for a change.

It was time to find out.

VIOLET
No. I don't want to right now.

Violet knew he'd reply quickly, so she turned up the radio to listen. She leaned her head back, closing her eyes, letting the vibration alert her to a new message instead of glaring at the screen until it popped up. It wasn't long.

TANNER
Violet Im really sorry. Please come over so we can talk please.

Her nose wrinkled, contorting into a frown. She seemed to recall a time she wanted to talk to him and he simply walked away with Neil at his side. It took quite a bit of self-control not to bring that up as she typed her next message.

VIOLET
Honestly, talking is not going to fix this. There is no reason you could give me that will just make this go away.

TANNER
…You think we should break up?

VIOLET
Yes. I have some stuff to figure out.

Her words were finite, confident. It felt good to express what she really thought. She exhaled deeply, like she was breathing out the months of built up tension from playing a part she didn't fully understand. It was so easy, finally being herself.

The screen still shone brightly from her lap as she noticed a series of dots indicating Tanner's response was coming. They disappeared and reappeared, playing a game of hide-and-seek until another short message replaced them.

TANNER
Im sorry. It was stupid. I deleted everything. Your right to be mad, I just hope you can forgive me.

*You're**, Violet imagined typing, but she chose not to respond. Instead, she dropped her phone into the cup holder, shifted into drive, and rolled along out of the parking lot. The basketball players were just getting in their cars to leave as well, what perfect timing.

The streets in the little suburban town were surprisingly empty on her drive home, like a long drive through the country. No red lights lingered too long, or pile-ups at the signs in her neighborhood. The trip was easy, and the sunlight reflected from patches of untouched, white snow along the sidewalks. Every color was visible in the sky, blues, purples, pinks, oranges. The ground reflected the sky so beautifully, surrounding the world in a glow of pastel rainbow lights, softened by clouds, warmed by slivers of sun.

Violet hummed along to the radio, her feather-light feeling had returned. She never thought a break-up would feel so positive and eye-opening, world opening even. She'd gone so long expecting their relationship would hold all the answers to what she didn't understand about herself, but all it did was cause more heartache.

This was how it was meant to be; everything had fallen into place.

She pulled into her driveway, and slowed to a stop, but she didn't turn the car off yet, something caught her eye.

"Dad?" Violet called, rolling her window down and shouting to Mr. Gray, who was delicately wrapping a string of Christmas lights around his forearm to stuff into a green plastic box, neatly stacked on top of several others, lining the walls of the garage, leaving the floor completely spotless.

"Hey, sweetie!" Mr. Gray called to her, waving as he clicked the top of the box into place. "I finally cleaned the garage today! What do you think!?" He was so proud of himself, Violet could tell. The look on his face seemed reminiscent of what she felt just then as well.

She couldn't stop herself from smiling and laughed, sticking both thumbs out her window for him to see, letting a cold breeze whisk into her window.

"Well, come on in! I cleared it out for you," he screamed.

Violet smirked and rolled her window up and lifted her foot off the brake, pulling slowly into the garage for the first time. She twisted her key and pulled it from the ignition, stepped out outside and scanned the garage in awe.

"It looks awesome, dad," she said, still in disbelief as she stepped on the concrete floor that only that morning was hidden by landscaping tools she wasn't sure her father had ever used.

Mr. Gray put his fists on his hips, admiring his job well done. He sighed pleasantly and said to Violet, "Finally got a spot in the garage. How's it feel?"

The answer was easy. "Feels good," she said. "Seriously, so good."

ACKNOWLEDGEMENTS

Writing this book, for me, was a long time coming and there are several amazing people I'd like to thank for their help and support as I finally made this project a reality.

First and foremost, I would like to shout-out Ashley Murdock. I'm not sure she knows that she's the one who helped me understand my own asexuality, but certainly, she does now. Without this understanding, I'm not sure this story would have ever been possible, because I'd still be where Violet was in the beginning, struggling to put my feelings into words.

Next, I'll be acknowledging Sarah Farris, Rachel Harris, Ashleigh Irvins, Lindsey Hinkel, and Megan, my squad of beta readers who really helped me pull together the details, clarify how to spell some characters' names, and make sure the ending was satisfying for potential readers. Their comments were wonderfully constructive and positive. It really gave me the confidence I needed to publish.

Then, we have my editor, Casey. I cannot thank her enough for fixing every tense switch, every piece of rogue punctuation, and every rambling mess that was a run-on. (and I know there were a lot!)

On a more personal level, I'd like to thank the collection of close friends who support me through every wild project or endeavor without question.

Firstly, my mother, Kelly, who after keeping my first book a secret from her and not my sister, was the first person I told about this one only a week after starting it. Then, of course, my sister, Miranda, who constantly rises above any and all trouble that comes her way, making her one of the strongest and most persevering women I have ever met, like a real-world Jess.

The handful of friends who always engaged with my updates and kept me going even though the most difficult writing draughts—Chrissy Margevicius and Ben Essex.

The love of my life, Nick Kemper, for sitting quietly beside me every morning I wrote and always understanding every time I said, "Wait! Just let me finish this last line; I'm almost done. I promise!" His patience with me is unmatched.

And finally, I want to take this paragraph to acknowledge every person who had a significant impact on me in high school. They surely recognized some details throughout the text as I pulled a lot from my own personal experiences to write it. I won't be naming names, but you know who you are and I appreciate all that you've done to contribute to my art.

Until the next one!